randall
& hopkirk
{deceased}

randall & hopkirk {deceased}

the files

andy lane

introduction by charlie higson

BOXTREE

First published 2001 by Boxtree
an imprint of Pan Macmillan Ltd
Pan Macmillan, 20 New Wharf Road, London N1 9RR
Basingstoke and Oxford
Associated companies throughout the world
www.panmacmillan.com

ISBN 0 7522 2356 9

1 2 3 4 5 6 7 8 9

A CIP catalogue record for this book is
available from the British Library.

Designed and typeset by
Dan Newman/Perfect Bound Ltd
Colour reproduction by
Aylesbury Studios
Printed and bound in Great Britain by
Bath Press

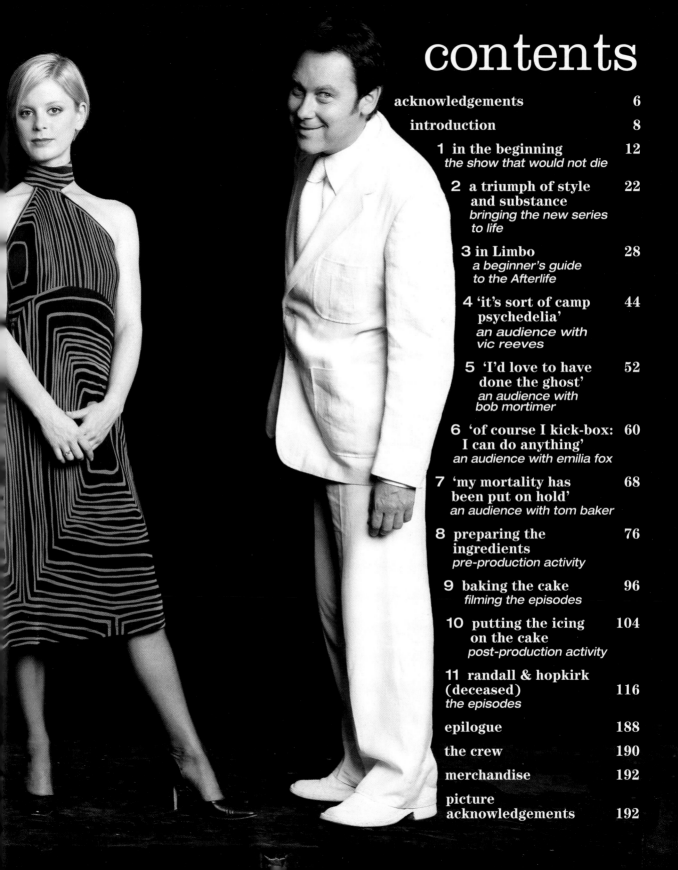

contents

acknowledgements

Filming a series as complicated as *Randall & Hopkirk (Deceased)* is a team business. And it's a large team – larger than you might think.

Imagine a film camera pointing at the three main characters – Jeff Randall, Marty Hopkirk and Jeannie Hurst – as they stand in the offices of the detective agency, Jeff arguing with Jeannie, Marty arguing with Jeff. These are the most obvious members of the team: the actors playing the parts. Now imagine that the camera is swivelling round to show you the people standing behind it. There's the director, the cameraman, the make-up artists, the lighting engineers, the sound engineers, the continuity girls and so many others, each one keeping as quiet as possible, moving as little as possible, while the actors are performing. And there are other members of the team whose jobs have already finished when the film starts rolling – the script writers, the storyboard artist, the set designers, the construction crews, the people who make, or find, the costumes. After the film has been developed there's a whole range of post-production staff: the editors who splice the scenes together, the special effects technicians who take the film and change it within their computers... And above it all, managing the process from beginning to end, there's the producer and the executive producer, along with their production staff, ensuring that the entire thing runs according to plan and that work carried out by the various members of the team comes together smoothly.

It is, as we said, a very big team.

During the writing of this book, we've tried to talk to people at every stage of the process. We've talked to the show's creators, writers and producers, its actors, its designers and technicians. We've visited the set, we've been on location and we've sat in darkened offices watching rough images flickering on screens. We've talked to people in bars, pubs, mobile homes and restaurants. We have dipped our fingers in every aspect of production over the past two years.

We would like to thank in particular the following people who generously agreed to be interviewed – sometimes at great length, and several times: Simon Wright, Charlie Higson, Vic Reeves, Bob Mortimer, Emilia Fox, Tom Baker, Grenville Horner, Simon Waters, June Nevin, David Arnold, Gareth Roberts, Mike Nicholson, Matthew Holben, Rod Woodruff and Andy Smart. Quotes from them are scattered throughout the book.

As well as the people listed above, we would also like to thank a number of others who made the writing of this book a great deal easier than it might have been. At Working Title Television, Sophie Siegle, Charlotte Frings and Paul Bennett have been amazingly efficient and friendly. At Double Negative, Anthony Bluff was wonderfully helpful in providing examples of their stunning work on the special effects. At Boxtree, Katy Carrington and Gillian Holmes steered the project with a firm but fair hand. Within the writing team, Richard Topping made an early exit but left behind some great material and, most importantly of all, Dan Newman's design has been the core element that has pulled the various components of this book together into a coherent whole. Thanks to everyone.

introduction

By Charlie Higson

May 18th 1999. A blue sky with fluffy white clouds. Birds tweeting in the trees. It's an old-fashioned English spring morning in an old-fashioned English churchyard. Suddenly there's a giggle and six gorgeous teenage nymphs, wearing very little except skimpy, diaphanous silks, skip into the sunlight and come prancing up the path, strewing flower petals in all directions.

'Cut. Okay, let's go again, and this time can you all try to keep in time with each other? Thank you.'

We are in St Peter's churchyard in Tandridge for the first day of shooting on the new *Randall & Hopkirk (Deceased)* starring Vic Reeves and Bob Mortimer. Some sixty-odd people are assembled here – camera operators, lighting technicians, sound engineers, designers, make-up artists, costume assistants, actors… Most of them don't know each other, and there's a certain nervous tension in the air. What's it going to be like? What's going to happen over the next fourteen weeks of filming? Will Vic and Bob remember their lines? Will the white suit stay white? And who the hell's that over there? The heavily pierced, leather-clad bloke on the huge motorbike…? (Turns out it's Kevin, the unit nurse.)

These and many other questions occupy me perhaps more than anyone else; after all, I've written the damn thing, I'll be directing one episode, I'm appearing in all of them and I've somehow ended up producing the show as well. So, if it all goes horribly wrong I guess I'll have to take most of the blame.

But I don't have time to brood too much about all this because right now there's work to be done.

Mark Mylod, the director, is setting up a shot in the medieval church porch. Our two detectives, Jeff Randall and Marty Hopkirk come charging in, on the trail of a mysterious woman in red. But she's disappeared and the door's locked. No problem; Marty's a ghost: he can simply walk through it, can't he?

Marty rushes up to the door and… slams painfully into it.

This is our first experience of filming the ghost, and, ironically, we are shooting an episode where he loses his powers and can't pass through solid objects any more. So the first thing Vic gets to do is bang his head against a heavy wooden door, under the watchful eye of the local vicar, played by Richard Durden.

But at least it's a relatively easy day. With Marty very much solid and visible, we don't have to wheel out all the effects crew and film endless permutations of each shot; plus Vic gets a chance to do one of the things he's best at – physical comedy.

This is what filming's always like: although it has an internal logic of its own, to an outsider it can sometimes seem completely random, if not perverse.

For instance we're shooting the last episode in the series first.

This is partly down to the availability of locations (most of the village exteriors will be shot in the perfectly preserved National Trust village of Lacock in Wiltshire – standing in for the sinisterly nice village of Hadell Wroxted), but it also gives Vic and Bob a chance to warm up and settle into their characters before we film the opening episode.

Above: Charlie Higson as seen by Vic Reeves.
Right: Producer/director/writer Charlie Higson turns his hand to the job of cameraman as well.
Below: 'Weird but fun.'
Opposite: The nymphs at prancing practice.

I've worked with Vic and Bob in one form or another a great deal over the years and can honestly say that it's all been fun – weird, but fun. In the process I've built up a store of priceless memories that time shall not dim – from the early days on stage at the Albany Empire in Deptford, playing things like a man with twenty-foot-long trousers or Tanita Tikaram (and having tart lemon squirted repeatedly in my eye), to helping out on their first TV shows as Mister Melons Goes To Chicago, or Hats Off To Harry Nielson, or even occasionally standing in for Bob as The Man With A Stick. Later I went on to co-produce *The Smell of Reeves and Mortimer*, where I also made the odd appearance (with the emphasis on 'odd'), usually in my underpants. In fact the very first time I did Swiss Toni was with them. They played the Bra-Men and I very unprofessionally tried to keep a straight face. Ah, the memories – appearing as a male stripper on *Shooting Stars* and nearly being assaulted by Lynn Perry in the process, laughing the hardest I've probably ever laughed in

my life at the Club Soda in Montreal as they performed a talking-crab routine to an utterly bemused Canadian audience…

And I didn't know it that day in Tandridge, but over two series of *Randall & Hopkirk* I'd build up another store of priceless memories that time shall not dim – playing a man who's lost his dog and laughing uncontrollably again until both Bob and I end up having to deliver our lines to a pillow; sitting in a pub in Clovelly, Devon, watching in horror as Ford Kiernan, the Scottish actor, teaches Vic how to eat a wine glass; trying not to laugh when the stuntman accidentally punches Bob full in the face during a fight scene; talking Vic down from the roof of a truck after a bad attack of low-altitude vertigo; listening to Tom Baker's insane stories and appearing on his *This Is Your Life* (something I never dreamed would happen when watching *Doctor Who* as a kid); getting told off in front of everybody by the divine Millie Fox for making stupid jokes while she's trying to get into the mood for a particularly sad scene; sitting with

Jane Walker, the fabulous make-up artist, and getting into yet another daft character; hearing the orchestra play David Arnold's extraordinary theme music for the first time in the recording studio; hanging out in the Winnebago with Vic and Bob while they try to convince me that prog rock is God's greatest gift to mankind…

But, as I say, I don't know about any of that on this sunny spring morning, all I know is that we have a punishing schedule to get through and anything can happen.

Luckily the first day goes swimmingly, which bodes well for the future. The sun shines, the girls look gorgeous, the white suit seems impervious to dirt, Vic and Bob remember their lines. (In fact it's Richard Durden, the vicar, who temporarily forgets his and swears magnificently, like only a classically-trained English actor can.) We get everything shot that we need and everyone goes home happy.

Perhaps, just perhaps, we might make it through this and have a great show on our hands.

IN
LOVING MEMORY
- OF -
HOPKIRK

in the beginning

the show that would not die

*T*he Odd Man... Police Surgeon... Public Eye... Remember them? The first was a cult series of the early 1960s that was spun off into two sequels – *It's Dark Outside* and *Mr Rose*. The second became *The Avengers*. The third was a detective series that ran for ten whole years. And yet they are lost. Gone. Almost completely forgotten apart from a few dedicated fans of the most cultish of cult TV.

Let's try another three, made around the same time. *The Persuaders. Man in a Suitcase. The Prisoner.* They need no description. They are available on video, they are shown regularly on terrestrial and cable television. What's different about them, what makes them memorable, is that they were scripted with a dash of humour and a sprinkling of fantasy. They were larger than life, and that's why they have lasted when others have faded.

Randall & Hopkirk (Deceased) was one of that batch of memorable series made in the golden age of television which lasted from 1967 to 1972. The simple story of a detective who solves crimes with the help of the ghost of his dead partner, it lasted for twenty-six episodes, but when the series failed to make its mark in the lucrative American market, it folded.

Fast forward thirty-odd years. Working Title Television (WTTV) – an independent television production company with a highly impressive track record – have obtained the rights to remake a number of television series from the Swinging Sixties. They cast around, wondering if any of them might work in the cynical new millennium.

And *Randall & Hopkirk (Deceased)* springs out at them.

Simon Wright, executive producer and President of WTTV, had initially envisaged the series as a straight thriller in the style of *Inspector Morse* or *Edge of Darkness*.

'When I first got the rights,' he explains, 'we commissioned Lise Mayer to write a script – she had previously co-written *The Young Ones*. We were going to take it down a really quite straight dark thriller line. Just imagine if somebody was a detective with a partner who died and came back – this man would be having brain scans and seriously doubting his sanity throughout the series. It would really be quite a hard-nosed thriller. So we started down that avenue, and somebody from *The Times* rang me up and asked me who were we thinking of casting. And I said, because the original was very tongue in cheek and very funny, that we'd potentially be looking at casting a comedian in the role of Marty Hopkirk.'

In fact, Simon was considering approaching Robbie Coltrane or Rik Mayall for the part of Marty. Television, however, like life, works on coincidence and luck as much as contacts and good planning. Comedy pair Vic Reeves and Bob Mortimer read the *Times* report, and it immediately struck the two that this was an ideal vehicle for them.

'It just felt right,' said Bob. 'It was a fun series in its day, and we just had this vision of us doing it.'

When Simon heard that Vic and Bob were interested in the show, the project suddenly had a sense of viability that wasn't there before. 'They come as a package,' he says. 'You know when you see Vic and Bob together that they've been friends for ever, that they have a history, that there's a body-language and an understanding between them that people can immediately relate to and understand. This was exactly what we needed with Jeff Randall and Marty Hopkirk because we need viewers to understand that these two characters, these lifelong friends, have a history to them.'

He did, however, have some concerns.

'I was worried that they would turn it into a sketch, a spoof, and that it would be good for twenty minutes,' he remembers. 'What I wanted to do was make it a long-running, perpetual series. They assured me that they really wanted to act, and that this was the vehicle for them. They wanted to change the way that people saw them.'

Simon sent the pair the early scripts, to get some initial feedback. 'The scripts were very dark and powerful,' Bob recalls. 'Very *Cracker* and *A Touch of Frost*. We didn't want to go down that route, so when Simon asked us who we'd think could create the sort of scripts we were after, Charlie Higson was the first name on the list.'

'Now Charlie never writes anything for anybody else, ever,' Simon Wright recalls, 'but I met him and he said yes, he would do it. So we started writing it, and Charlie just took it over and it became his baby.'

Although Charlie Higson had worked with Vic and Bob for many years he was, at that point, best known for his work on BBC TV's *The Fast Show*. What few people realized, however, was that he had also written a number of gritty novels. That ability to shift back and forth between darkness and light was to be crucial in the development of *Randall & Hopkirk (Deceased)*.

According to Simon: 'Charlie was interested in writing a prime-time family show that would amuse, excite, frighten and intimidate and go through the whole rack of emotions that a really

Jeff Randall (Bob Mortimer) is about to be preserved for posterity in the first episode of the series, 'Drop Dead'.

'When we first read the scripts,
we had me as Marty Hopkirk.'
Bob Mortimer

good drama would do – all in fifty minutes. And leave you laughing at the end. The big bonus is that he is really, really funny.'

Charlie Higson was persuaded to take on the controlling role of producer, as well as writing the first batch of episodes. It was a huge commitment of time and energy, and would essentially require him to dedicate two years of his life to the creation of five hours of television.

Having asked that Charlie Higson be brought on board, Bob Mortimer and Vic Reeves were intrigued to see what he would come up with. Except that there was some initial confusion over who was playing what.

'When we first read the scripts, we had me as Marty Hopkirk,' said Bob. 'What with Vic being taller and everything it just seemed to make sense, given the physical characteristics of the original actors. But then Charlie said he wanted to do it the other way round, with Vic as Marty and me as Jeff. When we had a read through it all made sense. There's a lot of manic energy in Marty –

what with him trying to learn how to be dead and struggling to use his powers to help his best mate and his fiancée, and Vic carries that energy really well. Once you go beyond the visual expectations of the two I think it works very well.'

Simon Wright, for one, was glad that his initial worries about the casting were unfounded.

'They worked very, very hard,' he says. 'These so-called "wild men of comedy", this dangerous duo, they were incredibly professional.'

'At first, it was hard to tell whether Vic and Bob were just constantly taking the piss out of you or whether they were being serious. Now I realise that they are constantly taking the piss out of you.'

Simon Wright, WTTV

There's a *Fast Show* sketch in which 'Arthur Atkinson' – the series' version of Max Miller and Arthur Askey – is seen acting in a worthy BBC production of a Samuel Beckett play. It's funny because of the incongruity, but that doesn't stop it from being accurate. From Morecambe and Wise (*The Sweeney*) to Billy Connolly (*Mrs Brown*), from Norman Wisdom (*Casualty*) to Michael Barrymore (*Bob Martin*), the old cliché of the clown who wants to play Hamlet is, like all clichés, based in truth.

But casting Vic Reeves and Bob Mortimer in a prime-time action adventure series… that was a bold decision. Despite repeated attempts to portray them as a genial double-act, their humour blends anarchy, surrealism and violence in a cocktail that is not to everyone's taste.

'We knew that some of the television audience were intimidated and almost frightened by Vic and Bob,' Simon Wright recalls, 'by their image and by their surreal humour. And people, when they don't exactly understand something, do sometimes get intimidated by it, and fear that they're the target of every joke. I did at first when I first met them. It was very hard to tell whether they were just constantly taking the piss out of you or whether they were being serious. Now I realize that they are constantly taking the piss out of you.'

Given Reeves and Mortimer's connections with the world of stand-up comedy, one might have expected to find them surrounded by familiar faces.

'There has been a temptation to put comedians into every episode of *Randall & Hopkirk (Deceased)*,' Simon admits. 'We really tried to shy away from that, partly because lots of other people want to be in it anyway, but also because we don't want it to become this elite little club. Because of Charlie's and Vic's and Bob's connections we could so easily fill it with everybody from *The League of Gentlemen*, *The Fast Show* and so on. We've been lucky with a lot of very high-quality actors, we've had Derek Jacobi, Charles Dance, Freddie Jones… so in a way we've got that balance right.'

Charlie Higson is very pleased with the quality of the acting in the series, but has some regrets over lost opportunities. 'There were a whole lot of people we wanted to use on the first series who were all working on *Gormenghast*,' he recalls: 'Stephen Fry, Richard Griffiths, Ian Richardson, Celia Imrie… We did get Celia Imrie in the end, which was fantastic. The other people we really wanted to get but just couldn't coax in were the people from Monty Python – John Cleese and Michael Palin in particular.'

Above: *Celia Imrie joined the cast as Professor McKern in 'Revenge of the Bog People'.*
Below: *Mark Gatiss and Steve Pemberton from* The League of Gentlemen *also made guest appearances as Sergeant Liddel and Inspector Large.*
Opposite top: *Vic Reeves and director Mark Mylod between takes during the filming of 'Drop Dead'.*
Opposite bottom: *Paul Whitehouse of* The Fast Show *guest-starred as the evil Sidney Crabbe in 'A Blast From the Past'.*

In a manner that can only be described as Hitchcockian, series producer and primary writer Charlie Higson has appeared in every episode so far. If you're looking out for him, this is who he is …

- a fisherman in 'O Happy Isle' (1)
- a Northern art critic in 'Drop Dead' (2)
- sinister civil servant Bulstrode in 'Paranoia' and 'Pain Killers' (3)
- a man reading a newspaper on a park bench in 'The Best Years of Your Death' (4)
- a cannabalistic villager in 'A Man of Substance' (5)
- a patient suffering from fits at a sanatorium in 'Mental Apparition Disorder' (6)
- a hotel guest in 'Whatever Possessed You' (7)
- a man who wants Jeff to locate his lost dog in 'The Glorious Butranekh' (8)
- a thug who comes to a nasty end in 'Two Can Play at That Game' (9)
- a museum security guard in 'Revenge of the Bog People' (10)
- Gomez the fey barman in 'A Blast From The Past' and 'Marshall & Snellgrove' (11)

a triumph of style and substance

bringing the new series to life

Before Vic Reeves and Bob Mortimer, there were Kenneth Cope and Mike Pratt. Before Emilia Fox there was Annette André. Before Tom Baker there was... well, there wasn't anyone. The point being, before the new *Randall & Hopkirk (Deceased)* there was an original version – one that is still remembered with some fondness today.

Producer and writer Charlie Higson is very clear about the reasons why memories of the original linger on when so many other series of the time have died a death. 'The attraction was that it was a very good central idea for a show: two detectives, one of them is dead and the only one who can see him is his partner. There's something very appealing about it, especially to kids. It's like having an invisible friend. Or it's a bit like having a superpower – you've got someone who can go places and see things and report back to you that nobody knows about.'

'There was a sort of dinginess to it ... it was all quite downbeat.'
Charlie Higson

The plots of the original series revolved around fairly mundane elements – thefts, murders, body-guard duties. While other ITC series such as *Department S* and *The Persuaders* did their best to break out of the strait-jacket of naturalistic drama, the original *Randall & Hopkirk (Deceased)* seemed determined to break back in. Despite its limitations, people seemed to like it.

Charlie is not, however, one of those people who view the past through nostalgia-tinted spectacles. 'At the risk of offending anybody who was involved in the original series,' he says, 'it wasn't that great. It was made very cheaply and quickly, and for various reasons they couldn't really capitalize on the central idea. The special effects were fairly primitive, they were limited in what they could do, and I believe that after the first few episodes they got into trouble for dealing too much with the implications of one of the characters being dead, for dealing flippantly with death. I think there was a lot more religious pressure on them. So they steered it towards being basically a fairly straight detective series.'

The over-riding impression left by the original series is that, apart from the seedy offices of the detective agency, it took place almost entirely in hotel corridors, anonymous apartments and warehouses, with the occasional excursion into the Elstree back lot for variety.

'There was a sort of dinginess to it,' Charlie agrees. 'It was all quite downbeat and, well, while it wasn't exactly cheap-looking, it wasn't expensive-looking either. It wasn't something like *The Avengers*, which was an absolute classic and was very stylish and had a lot of memorable bits and memorable characters. A lot of people can't even remember who the original actors were.'

Left: *Talking to yourself is the first sign of madness, and Jeff Randall certainly did a lot of that in the original series. A worried Jeannie (Annette André) looks on.*

Opposite: *The new* Randall & Hopkirk (Deceased) *paid tribute to the 1970s version by dropping in references to the original. Here, through the wonders of modern computer effects, the original Jeff Randall (Mike Pratt) appears to be a reticent presence in the Limbo Bar on Marty's first visit there.*

'One of the things we used to talk about right up front,' Simon Wright reveals, 'was that we wanted the new series to be like *The Cat and the Canary* – the Bob Hope film from 1939 – which was two things simultaneously. It's a very tense, dark thriller, but it's also very funny. That was always our benchmark: one second you're laughing your head off and the next second you really are quite frightened.'

It took some time to persuade the BBC of the merits of this approach, however.

'When we started,' Charlie Higson recalls, 'the BBC said, "You will make it a police/detective thing, won't you, because people understand that." And I said, "It's Vic and Bob and one of them's a ghost. Do you really want to be doing *The Bill*?"'

In fact, 'doing *The Bill*', as he puts it, was about the furthest thing from Charlie's mind.

'I get very bored by standard, realist drama,' he says. 'There were few more depressing sounds as a child than the theme tune to *Coronation Street*. That whole area of dull reality just leaves me

completely cold. As a child I'd always loved things that had more of a fantasy feel to them.'

Once the bold strokes had been put on paper – the decision to walk the line between humour and horror – the producers and the actors could then fill in some of the detail. The key possibilities quickly became apparent to Charlie. 'You could perhaps try and go into it a bit more than they did in the original,' he explains, 'explore a bit more about what it means to be dead and where Marty goes when he's dead, make more of the love triangle, make Jeannie much more of a central character, and try some more outrageous plots.'

For the new *Randall & Hopkirk (Deceased)* to truly succeed, it had to do something that the old one conspicuously failed at: crack the foreign marketplace. The original did its best not to look British, and ended up not looking like anything. The new version had taken a different tack.

'I went to great lengths to try and reduce any references that were specific only to English audiences,' Charlie says, 'in terms of references to

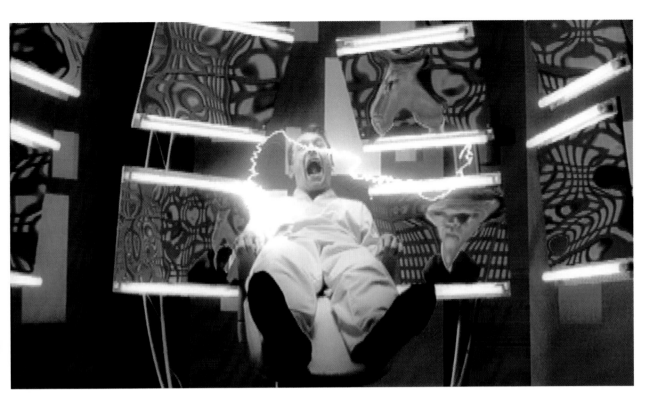

television shows or Alan Titchmarsh, but I was playing on American tourist ideas of what England is like. We did a crusty old public school, we did a charming little rural village... so I was trying to make it a recognizable England and then explore what was wrong with these places.'

If he had to sum up the style and the appeal of the new series in one or two sentences, Simon wouldn't have any problem.

'There are certain themes about the series,' he says: 'the agent provocateurs are always crazy, and Vic and Bob are quite definitely the worst detectives you've ever seen in your life.'

Charlie, too, has no doubts about the style of the series.

'In a sense it's more a kind of James Bond series: James Bond doesn't really do much spying, he just goes on adventures. I wanted to set the characters on adventures, and the private detective angle is just an excuse to put them into situations where they can sort of solve a mystery but more save the world.'

Opposite top: *The sets of the new show are an important part of its stylish and unique look. Taking its cue from, among others, 1960s and '70s TV and film styles, the design teams have created sets that blend these influences with a totally modern vision.*
Above and right: *The look and feel of James Bond adventures provide both a dramatic and visual influence in the making of the series.*

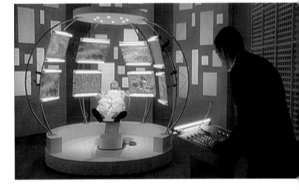

in Limbo

a beginner's guide to the Afterlife

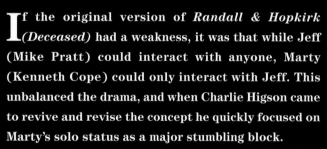

If the original version of *Randall & Hopkirk (Deceased)* had a weakness, it was that while Jeff (Mike Pratt) could interact with anyone, Marty (Kenneth Cope) could only interact with Jeff. This unbalanced the drama, and when Charlie Higson came to revive and revise the concept he quickly focused on Marty's solo status as a major stumbling block.

'I always felt, when I watched the original, that we needed to see where Marty goes when he isn't on earth,' Charlie Higson says. 'To my mind that was the great hole in the concept of the original.'

The solution was twofold. Firstly, Marty had to have somewhere to go when he wasn't with Jeff. That place was Limbo – the ever-shifting home of those lost souls who were still somehow tied to their past lives. Secondly, Marty had to have someone else to talk to. That someone was Wyvern, the avuncular mentor who helps him come to terms with his new spiritual status and tries – with difficulty – to teach him how to use his powers.

29

Wyvern

Who – or what – is Wyvern? We know nothing about his life on Earth before he arrived in Limbo, if indeed he had a life. Is he a denizen of the spiritual realm, a higher power who visits Earth from time to time but has never actually been born and died there? Or is he a mortal, like Marty, who has been left in Limbo to help other souls as some kind of penance, not allowed to move on until his sins have been expiated?

Wyvern's job is as some strange kind of supernatural personal fitness trainer. With some souls he enables them to come to terms with their death, allowing them to pass on to a higher realm. With the ones who are stuck in Limbo, associated with a Chosen One back in the human realm, he provides on-the-spot advice and helps them to realize the full potential of their powers. And, of course, nobody knows the full potential of Wyvern's own powers.

There are hints in his first appearance ('Mental Apparition Disorder') that Wyvern isn't quite what he seems, and in 'The Glorious Butranekh' he strongly indicates to Marty that appearances are meaningless in Limbo, that the mind creates its own reality. The avuncular figure that we see may just be how he wants to be seen by Marty, the kind of figure that Marty would best respond to. His true form may be much more horrific…

We know little of Wyvern's abilities, even after thirteen episodes, but we do know he is a truly terrible poet. His poetic incompetence has been made into an integral part of the series, given that his kindly rhymed instructions on how to manage the Afterlife leave poor Marty more confused than enlightened, and lead directly to his remaining on Earth with Jeff.

Wyvern: 'This is not what I really look like.'

Marty: 'And what do you really look like?'

Wyvern: 'You don't want to know, Marty. Believe me, you don't want to know.'

Opposite top: An original sketch of Wyvern's daemonic alternative persona – drinking tea!
This page: Matt Lucas as Wyvern's new student, Nesbit, joined by Tom Baker and Vic Reeves for 'Revenge of the Bog People'.

During the thirteen episodes of Randall & Hopkirk (Deceased), Marty has demonstrated some pretty phenomenal powers. They include the ability to:

● enter the realm of computer data and retrieve information ('A Blast From the Past' and 'O Happy Isle') – 1
● pass through solid objects ('Paranoia') – 2
● literally enter people's heads and control their actions ('The Best Years of Your Death') – 3
● appear on computer screens and TVs (various) – 4
● communicate with Jeff via the telephone ('Drop Dead')
● move objects by will power ('Mental Apparition Disorder' and 'Paranoia')
● imitate voices ('Mental Apparition Disorder')
● produce very smelly ectoplasmic wind ('Paranoia')
● shrink people's shoes ('Whatever Possessed You')
● change his form ('Pain Killers')
● smash things by singing ('O Happy Isle')
● steal spirit from a sleeping Jeff ('Revenge of the Bog People')

'That's fantastic – the ability to look constipated!'

Jeff

987,345,802

Limbo

Although Marty spends a lot of his time in Limbo (it's apparently the only place he can go, apart from wherever Jeff happens to be on Earth) we never get to find out much about it directly. What we do discover is glimpsed in the background or dropped into conversations, and even then it's often ambiguous and fragmentary. Limbo is, fittingly, a place of mystery, a place created by the minds that inhabit it. And, given the state of Marty's mind, that's a frightening thought.

The various aspects of Limbo sometimes seem like pieces of a jigsaw puzzle, and there's no picture on top of the box to help make sense of them. We know why souls arrive in Limbo – someone has died – and we have a pretty good idea that there are three places a soul can go on to. They can hang around in Limbo and head back to the mortal realm for short periods, if there is something they have left undone and if they have a special person on Earth – their Chosen One – to anchor them (although, as Wyvern explains in

835,808

'The Glorious Butranekh', Marty's own return was due to a mistake on the spiritual paperwork). They can go onward and upward to a better place – the Afterlife – like Marty's dad in 'A Blast from the Past'. Or they can be dragged down to a rather nasty realm like Harry Wallis in the same episode. But what are the rules? What does one have to do to go up, or down?

Limbo itself is home to a restless and shifting population of souls who aren't moving in any direction. It has its different environments, its regions, its landmarks. There are some places, like the Limbo Bar, where you might almost believe you're back on Earth. There are others, such as the Pit of Oblivion, where souls are torn apart in eternal fire, and the Waiting Room, where those who have drifted apart from their Chosen Ones wait... and wait... and wait...

Limbo, it has to be said, doesn't follow normal laws of logic. The street where Wyvern 'lives', for instance, stretches on for ever. Wyvern's 'house' is Number 987,345,804. Are there trillions of other spirits like Wyvern, each with his or her own set of students? Are the rest of the 'houses' occupied by spirit families who bang on the walls when Marty makes too much noise? Or is the whole thing just a spin-off from Marty's mind, a visual representation of what he subconsciously expects to see? Or fears to see?

Nothing can be relied upon in Limbo. Even the geography shifts around while you're not looking. Marty seems to have easy access to Wyvern's street and room for most of the first series before encountering the huge Limbo sign in 'A Blast from the Past', but in the next episode – 'A Man of Substance' – the sign has become the entrance to Limbo itself, and Marty can't even get past it to find Wyvern. There are no maps, and yet the spirits seem to find their way to where they are going. Or perhaps where they are going finds its way to them...

Nothing is permanent in Limbo; everything is in flux. And yet some things seem to persist. Gomez, the barman, holds down a permanent job, despite the occasional gangster knocking his head off, and Wyvern persists in his training, helping new souls to ascend. Or helping them steer clear of the alternative...

Above: *After he dies, Marty finds himself on an endless street in Limbo, about to encounter his supernatural mentor, Wyvern, in 'A Blast From the Past'.*
Right: *The Waiting Room is where souls go when they have lost contact with their Chosen Ones – either through a 'drifting apart' or by choice.*

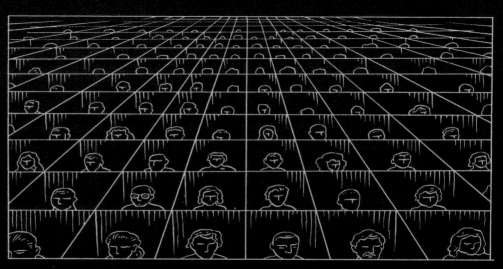

In the strange, shifting surroundings of Wyvern's room, Marty first learns to use his powers (above). But it is not just Wyvern's domain, as Marty finds out when Limbo's guardian pawns burst through the walls in pursuit of Sebastian Snellgrove (opposite).

Wyvern's room

'I created all this so you would feel at home,' says Wyvern, reclining in his armchair in an ornate and fusty library during his first encounter with Marty ('Mental Apparition Disorder'). But this is no ordinary library. Despite the high, vaulted arches and inset coves, despite the clocks, the books, the pictures, and the statues, there's something not quite right about it.

Like Wyvern himself, the room is not quite what it seems. As befits a figment of the imagination, the room shifts in and out of reality, the walls gently undulating and waving like tall grasses in a breeze. It's as if Wyvern can't be bothered to concentrate on fixing it: all the elements are present, but they just drift around willy-nilly. Or perhaps he prefers it that way. Perhaps he delights in the uncertainty of never knowing where a particular book, or bowl of fruit, has ended up.

By an effort of will, Wyvern can alter his surroundings, replacing them with something more soothing, if called for, or something much more worrying. He demonstrates this to Marty at one point, first replacing the room with an airport runway complete with screaming aircraft, and then with a rather more terrifying location – what appears to be a castle drawbridge complete with a giant, spider-like monster.

It's not only Wyvern's will-power that can affect the room, however. When 1950s gangster Sidney Crabbe escapes from Limbo's Waiting Room and encounters Marty in the Limbo Bar in the episode 'A Blast from the Past', he then intrudes into Wyvern's room, manifesting as a giant head that bursts through the wall. The Pawns that hunt down newcomers to Limbo in 'Marshall & Snellgrove' also enter without

> ## 'I created all this so you would feel at home.'
> ### Wyvern

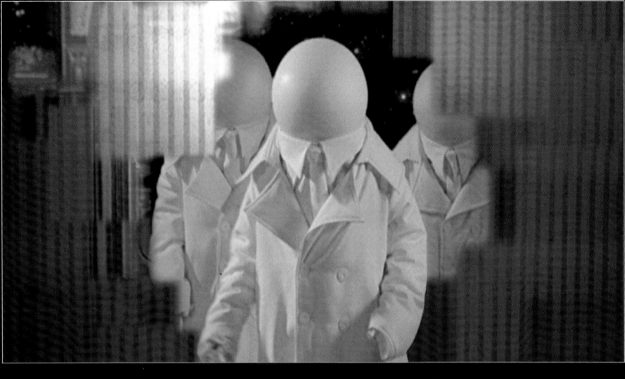

permission, and Wyvern seems powerless to stop them. It may be his room, but it's their rules.

In quieter moments, Wyvern enjoys a little undemanding sport. Cricket, for instance, or bowls, or fishing. He doesn't have to leave his room to do this: the walls appear to recede from him, allowing the room to encompass all the space he needs so that he can play without even moving from the spot. And it even provides an audience as well.

Comfortable and slightly old-fashioned on the surface, and yet shifting like a kaleidoscope underneath, Wyvern's room is a reflection of many things, but mostly of Wyvern himself.

The Limbo Bar

'Hello, duckie, welcome to Limbo,' says the barman. 'Care for a glass of champagne?'

It's his first time exploring the Afterlife, and Marty has arrived in the Limbo Bar. It has the appearance of a designer watering hole somewhere in London's West End – all stark angles, black backgrounds and harsh underlighting – but there's something disturbing about it, something not quite right. Perhaps it's the fact that the bouncer on the door only has half a face (the lower half). Perhaps it's the way the drinks don't taste of anything at all. Or perhaps it's the way the glasses tend to wobble in your hand unless you concentrate really, really hard.

The Limbo Bar, like the rest of Limbo, is an illusion. 'It doesn't exist,' the barman tells Marty. 'None of this is real, after all. It's just whatever you want it to be.'

The bar is patronized by a number of spirits, too bored to go anywhere else, who sit and drink and make small-talk whilst eternity creeps by. The spirits are patronized by Gomez, the barman whose slicked-back hair and pencil moustache give him the air of a *maître d'* from some 1940s William Powell and Myrna Loy movie. Gomez has seen it all. Nothing surprises him any more, not even having his head knocked off by ghostly criminal Sidney Crabbe in 'A Blast from the Past'. All he says is, 'Well, who got out of the wrong side of his coffin this morning, then?'

Despite the fact that the beer tastes like water, the conversation is dull and the barman condescending, Marty keeps returning to the bar. He finds Sebastian Snellgrove there in 'Marshall & Snellgrove', when the detective is killed by a bomb blast, and later discovers that Yuri – Felia's husband – has ended up there after sacrificing himself to bring back a Latvian war hero in 'The Glorious Butranekh'.

Perhaps, if one waits long enough, everyone comes to Gomez's bar, just as in *Casablanca* everyone comes to Rick's.

'It doesn't exist, sir. None of this is real, after all. It's just what you want it to be.'
Gomez the barman

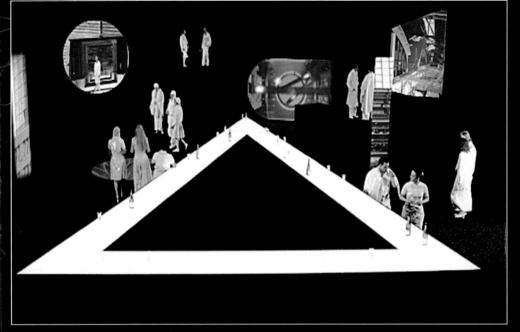

Many spirits pass through the Limbo Bar, from the confused Sebastian Snellgrove to the vicious Sidney Crabbe. But for all, the barman, Gomez, is always there to dispense philosophical wisdom and tasteless champagne.

Rhadamanthus-on-Sea: a place where spirits can 'get their act together'. Dicky Klein and Mrs Applegarth attempt to lure a vulnerable Marty into an eternal wet Sunday afternoon on Rhadamanthus Pier (below left).

Rhadamanthus-on-Sea

If Limbo is, as Wyvern suggests, an illusion created by the collective minds of all the souls who exist there, trapped between Heaven and Hell, then Rhadamanthus-on-Sea is the bit they came up with on a wet Sunday afternoon. It is, quite literally, the Last Resort, the long, dark Eastbourne of the soul. It's where spirits are sent when they fall out with the living companions who are keeping them from moving on. It is where ghosts go to die.

And when Marty and Jeff have an argument, and Marty suddenly finds himself estranged from his erstwhile partner, unable to communicate with him in any way, Rhadamanthus-on-Sea is where he finds himself.

'This is a place where people are brought in times of spiritual crisis,' Wyvern tells Marty. 'Far from the madding crowd. A quiet little place, unpretentious, where you can "get your act together".'

Marty has to reflect on the causes of the split and try to make things right again, but the little corner of Limbo in which he now finds himself isn't exactly conducive to thought. In fact, it's more like he's already been judged and sentenced.

Rhadamanthus-on-Sea is, quite literally, a ghost town. Like some ghastly seaside resort, shunned by tourists and inhabited only by those too weak to escape, it exudes a malign presence. A miniature golf course, an esplanade along which baby carriages blindly wheel themselves, a pier that seems to go on forever, occupied by mewling, gibbering spirits: it's a nightmare location poised between light and dark, between order and chaos, between sanity and madness.

The spirits Marty finds there are the flotsam and jetsam of the spirit world, cast up on the beach after they have argued violently with their Chosen Ones. Dicky Klein, once part of the music-hall act D. Klein and Fall, now trudges through one half of a comedy banter act, waiting vainly for an answering response. Mrs Applegarth runs a seedy hotel, eternally cursing the memory of her lost husband while her guests gradually forget the names of the people they left behind. And then, softly and suddenly, they vanish away.

Not everything on the other side is sweetness and light, warns Wyvern. There are dark forces at work. Watching. Waiting.

Rhadamanthus-on-Sea is a trap, a lure for weakened souls, created by forces that wish to snare the unwary and to exploit divisions wherever they find them for their own unfathomable ends. Wyvern can't interfere: all he can do is hope that Marty can sort out his differences with Jeff before Marty, too, finds himself mewling and gibbering on the pier. The infinite, eternal pier.

Limbo is full of these dreadful places, where unwary souls are at risk. And Wyvern, despite his powers, seems curiously powerless. There are rules. There are more powerful spirits even than him. 'I cannot be seen to intervene too directly,' he says. 'Choice has bought you here. I can only offer you more choices.'

If Mrs Applegarth and Dicky Klein and the Grand Hotel are only one of the choices open to Marty, what were the others like?

'it's sort of camp psychedelia'

an audience with vic reeves

'**I**'ve always enjoyed playing Marty. I find him a cheeky character, an appealing character and I fully enjoy pointing.'

Jim Moir, known as Vic Reeves to the world at large, leans back in his lavishly equipped caravan and draws on a cigarette. He's wearing white boots, white socks, white trousers and a white polo-neck jumper. Even the cigarette is white. If it wasn't so obvious that he was filming for *Randall & Hopkirk (Deceased)* he'd look like a refugee from the 1970s disco scene.

It's the last day of shooting on 'The Glorious Butranekh', which is also the final episode to be filmed for the second series. Away from the set and his regular foil Bob Mortimer, Vic is on the whole more serious and down to earth – ironic for someone who has spent much of the last two years playing a ghost who inhabits Limbo. 'This is good fun. I wouldn't know what to do if I wasn't doing this,' he sighs. 'You get used to getting up and having your breakfast made for you, and your lunch. Which is a joy really. From an idle man's point of view.'

He's increasingly enjoyed working on *Randall & Hopkirk (Deceased)* as the months have gone by, and has never regretted taking on the mantle of the dead detective. 'I saw the old series when it was first on, and I loved it,' he recalls. 'I think it was on a par with *The Man from U.N.C.L.E.* and *The Avengers*. Those British series were always quite camp.' The series was an influence on him early in his television career. 'During the very first *Big Night Out*, I wore a white suit, same as this, which I'd nicked off Marty Hopkirk, 'cos I thought it was a good look. And I think Bob and I probably started thinking about doing it then, but we never did anything about it. If I'd known then we were going to end up playing Randall & Hopkirk I'd have kept the suit and saved Charlie a few bob on the price of costumes.'

WTTV were, perhaps, taking something of a risk by casting two comedians in a semi-straight dramatic series – especially ones known for anarchic, apparently spontaneous comedy. One impression Vic is keen to dispel, however, is that he and Bob have suddenly had to become 'actors'. As he points out, the difference between the sort of work that the pair have done in the past, and filming a fifty-minute comedy drama is more a matter of scale than style. 'It's not at all different, when you think about it,' he argues. 'We've been acting in sketches. You don't act funny in sketches – you act straight to make them funny. It's all straight acting.' He looks down at his white suit and takes another drag at his cigarette. 'It's exactly the same as doing this. It's just another character.'

To establish that character took most of the first fifty-minute episode, which Vic frankly considers was not one of their best. 'It was quite hard doing the first episode,' he recalls, 'because it just had to set up the fact that I got killed. It wasn't really very exciting. It was a bit difficult, because you knew that you were putting probably the worst one on first.'

Above: Jeannie and Marty, engaged to be married, before Marty's fatal encounter with the bonnet of Annette Stylus's car.

However, he feels that the series has now found its niche. 'Now it's all set up, everyone knows who Jeff, Marty and Jeannie are, and you can take it further,' he points out. 'It's been very good. It's sort of camp psychedelia – this year we've got that sort of *Avengers* feel, with mannequins that move and spear you with umbrellas, and a huge Punch and Judy chasing people around. I'm looking forward to seeing how people react to that because I think that sort of camp psychedelic drama could become an important genre again. I also liked the way they spoke and reacted to each other: it's a sort of stylized flirtation.

'I think this series is better than the first – in fact it's very good indeed. There's more comedy in the stories, but there's more seriousness in them too. The drama has got a bit earthy, and gritty, but every one of these is quite fantastical, like the last episode of the first series. The first one this year is very frightening. But Marty's a bit lighter this series. It's not entertaining to watch him always complaining about being dead, so he has a bit more fun.'

The horizons of the series have expanded with the addition of new writers to the script roster for the second season. Vic and Bob have also been able to contribute to the scripts. 'Bob and me have had more of a free rein on the little set pieces and things that we do,' Vic says. This isn't to say that they have started ad-libbing when the cameras are rolling. 'No, we've been writing the dialogue beforehand,' he explains. 'There are

'During the very first *Big Night Out*, I wore a white suit, which I'd nicked off Marty Hopkirk 'cos I thought it was a good look.'

occasional bits of improvisation, but mainly we went through the scripts before we started filming and we thought of little things that we could do throughout.'

Marty Hopkirk's nature doesn't allow Vic that much direct interaction with the rest of the characters in an episode, unless he's being pursued by Paul Whitehouse's Sidney Crabbe in 'A Blast from the Past'. The same episode also provided Vic with some excitement, even if it was the sort he could do without. 'I suffer from very bad vertigo. I experienced the thrill of intense fear when I was six storeys up and had to shoot Paul Whitehouse. The look of fear on my face tells the whole story. That's not brilliant acting, that's sheer terror. For some reason Charlie managed to write a scene in pretty much every episode where I end up somewhere very high.'

> '**We're constantly told by Charlie to make it less camp, because we really ham it up a lot of the time.**'

Marty's main contact is with his spiritual mentor, Wyvern, and working on these scenes with Tom Baker, who brings Wyvern to larger-than-life, has been a particular joy. Vic's face lights up when he talks about his co-star. 'Me and Tom get on very well,' he says with a broad grin. 'He's fantastic. He's insane, but in a pleasant way. We're constantly being told by Charlie to make it less camp, because we really ham it up a lot of the time, and it all gets taken out at the end of the day. Whoever's directing it makes us do it again and again until we stop arsing around. Tom mucks around all the time, but I get the feeling he always has done. But he's always there, word perfect, and he'll always try different ways of doing things. I think that's the charm of Tom.'

Vic has also been particularly pleased by the way that Marty and Wyvern's relationship has shifted as the series has progressed. 'He's a bit cheekier now. He's getting a bit bored with me,' he maintains, 'so he sends me off to do tasks. But he's always got a wry grin, and he tricks me quite often.'

Although Vic claims that his working day as Marty simply consists of 'getting up there, doing it, and then you have your dinner,' he has found delight in some of the odd locations that have been used for the episodes. In 'Two Can Play at That Game', they ended up in a recently rediscovered old Music Hall in East London. 'That was great,' he enthuses, 'an amazing place. It was where Charlie Chaplin started, and Stan Laurel, and people like that. It was an amazing building – and it had a door that went through from the Music Hall into a pub, into a brothel, into a church. So you could do the circuit.' He grins wryly. 'You had an insight into how they spent their weekends – or probably every night.'

That episode guest-starred Roy Hudd, an acknowledged expert on the Music Hall tradition. 'He goes on endlessly about it, which is quite interesting,' Vic says fondly. 'It was good fun working with him. He stands very close to you when he talks, which is quite disconcerting. Everything's a bit conspiratorial with him.'

Hudd is by no means the only major name to grace the series, but, as Vic points out, 'once you've been in this business for a while, it's less amazing to work with somebody who people see on the television and think of as huge stars, whether it's Derek Jacobi or Charles Dance. In any case, I can do an entire episode and not meet them. I did very little with Derek – I think he attacked me, but that's the nature of what I am. I don't often get much contact with people.'

Opposite: *'The Glorious Butranekh'. Marty and Jeff find themselves in Latvia, first in a seedy bar, then deep in the forest of the Butra cult, trying to unearth clues to baby Marty's disappearance.*

It's clear that Vic would prefer Marty to have more direct involvement with the action, and interact with more than just Jeff and Wyvern. 'I stand back and watch the action scenes with jealousy,' he says, 'because I'd quite like to leap in and punch someone. I just stand around watching, and then do a bit of blowing... but it does look good at the end of the day.' Although the casting means that he is wearing his coveted white suit, Vic wishes he could share a few of those fights. 'Bob gets more action. In the next series I want more powers. I want to create electricity and water, and stuff like that, instead of just blowing. Or I could have a fight with another ghost, 'cos there are some superb fight scenes and sword fights, but I stand back and watch, and eventually just blow something and win. I think if we can contrive me having some spectral battles, I'd prefer that more.'

So his fondest memories from shooting the series?

'Well... let's think now.' An evil gleam appears in his eye. 'When we were filming the other day and the press all came down – that was a particularly good day. I convinced them all that there was a burial mound in these woods that had been a clowns' training ground in the Middle Ages and there was a terrible clown disease and they all died and were all buried in this huge mound. They all went to take photographs of it. And I also sent them back up again because I told them George Peppard was buried up there, so they went up with their cameras to try and find the grave.'

He pauses. 'We just talk endless rubbish from dawn to dusk here,' he sighs, shaking his head.

'In the next series I want more powers. I want to create electricity and water.'

CHAPTER FIVE

'I'd love to have done the ghost'

an audience with bob mortimer

'**W**e were trying to pull the wool over people's eyes a bit, hoping we could just put the laughs to the back,' admits Bob Mortimer, as he looks back over the first two series of *Randall and Hopkirk (Deceased)*, in which he and Vic Reeves have taken on the serious roles of the detective duo.

It's not as if this is the first time that Bob's career has changed direction. Before teaming up with Vic Reeves, he was an apprentice at Middlesborough Football Club, then a solicitor, dedicating his time to 'taking on the Tories with the rate capping. I couldn't stand being a solicitor, but at least that was something I could believe in. Because you have to train for so long, it's very hard to convince yourself to be brave enough to leave. The only thing that could possibly have dragged me away from that awful world was something as bizarre as Michael Grade saying, "Would you like to go on telly?"'

Femme fatale *Lauren Dee (Jennifer Calvert)* is about to lead Jeff and Marty into a dangerous situation, namely the unusual village of Hadell Wroxted.

That, strangely, was exactly what happened – one day he and Vic were working at the Albany Empire, the next they were appearing on Channel 4. When they later moved to the BBC, they were searching for new formats and, as Bob recalls, 'They said, "What do you want to do?" and we blurted out, "What about *Randall and Hopkirk (Deceased)*? Why doesn't somebody do that?"'

Although nothing came of it at that time, a while later the idea re-emerged. 'I was reading the *Sunday Times* and I saw a little thing that said that Working Title had bought the rights to *Randall and Hopkirk (Deceased)*,' Bob recalls. 'So I phoned our manager and told her to give them a ring and say that we would do it. And they called our bluff.'

Like Vic, Bob had loved the show when he was growing up. 'It appealed to youngsters,' he says. 'It was scheduled quite early, so that there was a fifty-minute programme for you as a fourteen-year-old with glamorous people in it. It felt like, "Wow, this is a classy item."'

When it came to reinventing the series for the new millennium, Vic and Bob decided that they didn't want to write the scripts themselves, and suggested Charlie Higson for the job. 'We were aware that an expensive project like this wasn't for our indulgence,' Bob notes. 'I'm glad Charlie did it. If he does something, he goes for it in a really unpretentious way. He's supportive and never says anything just for the sake of it – he has the strength to go to media meetings and just keep his mouth shut because he doesn't have anything to say.'

Some of the changes to the original format were suggested by Bob. 'We did have the feeling that it had to be a Saturday night programme, not just for "Vic and Bob" fans, and not just for cult telly people to watch,' he maintains. 'We decided that we had to do something new that was really obvious, and I suggested that we should have an Obi-Wan Kenobi character. I came up with a few things – I can't resist fiddling with things, even when I've promised myself I'll keep my mouth

'I probably have to film about twice as much as Vic does, and it becomes a bit of a pain. Especially when he's sitting around in his caravan watching videos.'

'I've got a feeling that I'm probably not an actor.'

shut! But I don't feel that it was my baby, or that I'm going to do the characters that I think are funny, so I don't feel so personally involved in it.'

The biggest challenge that both he and Vic found during the initial batch of episodes was maintaining one character for such a long stretch of time. 'I've got a feeling that I'm probably not an actor,' Bob says. 'I do what I do what I do. I think we were both better on the second series. We asked our directors and Charlie to keep an eye on us, and we did have a try at trying to believe it more. But in the absence of a director telling us to be weepy, or really nasty – which never happened – I just do Jeff Randall as Bob Mortimer.'

Bob is occasionally frustrated by the necessity of keeping Jeff as a very straight, simple character. 'Charlie's tried to stick to this thing that there's a detective element to each episode,' he points out. 'We try to make the villains and the surroundings pretty off-the-wall, so I think Millie and I have to bed it down in reality a little – which is a bit of a

strain. I'm always jealous of the people who get the lead roles because they can let themselves go, whereas the lines that Charlie writes for Millie and me are to do with the plot. Every night when I was learning my lines I'd go through them to see if there was anything I could do with the words, but they were always things like, "Quick, Jeannie, we have to get to the brewery!" Someone's got to do them, and it does leave some room within a tight fifty minutes for some cracking performances from people like Hwyel Bennett.'

It was the arrival of director Metin Huseyin in series two that allowed Bob the luxury of working on his acting skills.

'Metin was keen on us thinking about who the people were. The very first rehearsal we had with him, rather than rehearse he spent the first hour asking me "Who is Jeff Randall? What does he like? What are his foibles?" I'm often just listening to people in scenes, and I can remember him saying, "Bob, can you *look* like you're listening?" And I said, "I *am* listening, I really *am*," and he

said, "No, you have to move your eyes when you listen." I said, "I *don't* move my eyes when I'm listening," and he said, "Well, do it anyway."'

This isn't to say that Bob has never been given an opportunity to show what he can do. He relishes pretending to be a teacher in 'The Best Years of Your Death', but he still finds it incredible 'what proper actors can do'. At the end of 'Pain Killers', Jeannie sees Marty Hopkirk for the first time since his death, and Bob recalls that 'Millie just started weeping. We didn't know that she was going to do that. But she had to work herself up for hours to cry like that.'

He is equally amazed at the fortitude and professionalism shown by guest star George Baker during the filming of 'O Happy Isle'. 'The weather was just awful, and they had him stood in a river,' he says. 'These livid shapes started appearing on his face. He was in a bad way, but he's a real trouper. I said to Charlie, "Are you sure we shouldn't just stop?"'

'O Happy Isle' began as one of Vic and Bob's suggestions to Charlie. 'As a challenge, we said, "Can we have one where someone turns people gay?" We saw an episode of something – it might have been *Randall and Hopkirk (Deceased)* – which had a quite camp bloke living on a houseboat. It was an image you often saw in those days. We wondered what he'd be up to – and decided that he'd be putting something in the water supply to turn people gay.'

They had plenty of other ideas, as Bob explains: 'We had daft ones – like, there was a bloke living in a semi-detached house somewhere, and he had a cockroach – a huge cockroach – that he bred little cockroaches from. He put them into the banks and butchers and so on, and they all had to shut down. There was one pest control company that seemed to be able to get rid of them – and of course it was his company.' He sounds crestfallen. 'Charlie didn't use any of them,' he says.

But Bob doesn't rule out the possibility of contributing scripts to future series. 'If there's another series, it means this one's been a hit,' he

'We didn't go the route of detective story ideas ...
like, there was this bloke and he had a cockroach –
a huge cockroach...'

points out. 'I'd be happy that we could make it our own world, and that we wouldn't have to worry about the detective thing. We could completely let go of the anchor and be really bonkers.'

Even then, the combination of Vic and Bob's humour with the set-up of *Randall and Hopkirk* wouldn't mean everything changed. '*Randall and Hopkirk* is set in the England that Vic's and my comedy has always existed in,' Bob explains. 'All the little characters that we do could live in those little villages. It's one of the things that has helped give the show an identity: the locations were good – English country houses and public schools. We prefer a village green to a council estate. And it's not that we don't like those places, it's just that we're in that other world when we create those characters.'

When they first spoke to Working Title, Vic and Bob assumed that Bob would play Marty Hopkirk. 'Everyone at the meeting felt quite the reverse, so we instantly said, "Yeah, you're so right – what were we thinking of?" But I wish I had played Marty. I'd love to have done the ghost. It's one of those impact things. I used to look forward to the ghost appearing in the original, and we have that factor in the new series as well – you want the ghost to appear.'

There's also a practical reason that Bob would love to swap roles: 'To be perfectly honest, I probably have to film about twice as much as Vic does, and it becomes a bit of a pain. Especially when he's sitting around in his trailer watching videos.'

But whichever role he's playing, Bob Mortimer knows that he is lucky. 'A lot of other people trod the same path that I did, and it didn't happen for them. Sometimes I feel that someone was smiling on me.'

'yes, of course I kick-box: I can do anything'

an audience with emilia fox

Filming is, as anyone who has ever seen it going on will tell you, one of the most boring things on Earth. There's a lot of standing around waiting for cameras to be moved by a fraction of an inch, for lights to be adjusted for the millionth time and for the director to adjust the position of every prop. Actors on set tend to stand around like people at a bus stop: not quite catching each other's eye and making desultory conversation while waiting for someone to shout 'Action!'

Which means that Emilia Fox, who seems to vibrate with enthusiasm, even after several hours filming under hot lights, is not your average actor.

'I'd never done anything like this before,' she says in a cavernous soundstage in Ealing Studios. Behind her, the cameras are shifted around to get a better angle on the offices of Randall & Hopkirk (Deceased)

Above: One of the many men who fall for Jeannie is rival detective Charlie Marshall (Shaun Parkes).
Below: In 'Drop Dead', Jeff and Jeannie wait for Marty to turn up for his wedding. And wait...

'I loved the fact she's an independent character ... she's got a bit of depth and mystery to her.'

Security Services, 'and I'd certainly never considered that I would end up working alongside people like Vic Reeves and Bob Mortimer.'

In the original version of the series, the part of Jeannie Hurst was a token female ornament, written as a stable reminder of the 'ordinary' world that Marty no longer belongs to and Jeff is half in and half out of since the death of his partner. In the new version, the last thing that could be said about Jeannie is that she is stable and ordinary. In fact, she is in many ways the most complex character in the series.

'I loved the fact that she stands on her own two feet as an independent character,' Emilia confirms. 'She's marked out as being a bit of a misfit, and has a great sense of looking forward, unlike Marty and Jeff, who – let's face it – are pretty hopeless detectives. But I think what I most liked was the fact that she wasn't in any way a cartoony type character. She's got a bit of depth and mystery to her.'

Of the four main members of the cast, Emilia Fox was the only one who had to audition. Vic Reeves and Bob Mortimer arrived on board before scripts were even written, and the part of Wyvern was written for, and offered directly to, Tom Baker. She certainly came in with an impressive set of acting credentials, having made her debut on British television as Georgiana Darcy in the 1995 BBC adaptation of *Pride and Prejudice* and gone on to appear in a number of plays and television series, including *The Cherry Orchard*, *Rebecca*, *Shooting the Past* and the critically acclaimed *Bright Hair*. Coincidentally, she was appearing at the Donmar Warehouse theatre with Charles Dance, who was to guest star alongside her in the first episode of the series, when she was asked to audition.

One might be forgiven for thinking that a classically trained actress might have misgivings when she found out that she would be playing 'straight man' to a pair of comedians, but that isn't how Emilia saw it.

'I can't wait to get back into Jeannie's shoes. Especially if I'm allowed to keep them this time.'

'It was a perfect combination because the boys have this deep understanding of how comedy works. I've got more confidence in what people might term "straight" acting, so we were able to feed off each other. But that doesn't mean Vic and Bob aren't actors. Quite the opposite actually. You watch some of their shows and they're banging out ten characters in half an hour. There's nothing different or less accomplished about that at all. Personally, I think that's the hardest thing in the world, and *Randall & Hopkirk* was no step into the unknown for either of them.'

The audition process was by no means a walk-over for Emilia, despite her experience. Simon Wright and Charlie Higson saw aproximately seventy actresses for the role of Jeannie, and Emilia didn't expect to get the part. In fact, the main reason she auditioned at all was in order to make new contacts in the business.

'I was thrilled to meet Charlie, which was all I was interested in really. After that, I figured the part had gone to someone else. I was very surprised when Charlie came back to see me a second time.'

She laughs, remembering what happened. 'At our second meeting Charlie casually asked if I could do any kick-boxing. I was really into getting the part by then, so I crossed my fingers behind my back and said, "Yes, of course I kick-box. I can do anything." Once I was offered the part and read through all the scripts I realized I was on shaky ground, so I had to get myself in shape frighteningly quickly. I signed up for the local health club and did a month of intensive workouts. It was pretty grim. I was doing these kick-boxing classes three nights a week for about two months.'

It shows. Jeannie's introduction in 'Drop Dead' had her decking Charles Dance, and there are numerous examples afterwards of her leaping forward to tackle the villains while Jeff gets tangled up in something. One of the most dramatic occurs in 'Paranoia', where she and actor Alexis Denisof go at it hammer and tongs in a

For the part of Jeannie, Emilia Fox had to learn how to kick-box and then perform convincing fight scenes.

hotel room while Jeff is supposedly tied to a bed next door.

'That was the longest workout I think I've ever had,' she says ruefully. 'It took over six hours to film that one sequence. It really pushed me to the limits.'

Someone passes by, carrying a large gilt chair that's needed for a scene with Wyvern later, and she steps out of his way.

'It's very difficult doing authentic fight scenes,' she adds, 'because your natural reaction is to try and miss your opponent by as much as possible. I mean, those high kicks can really hurt if you connect properly. But it has to look convincing and if you don't get the angle just right, it all looks terribly staged. We were completely exhausted by the end of it, but looking at the scene now I'm glad we made such an effort. It works really well, especially since I'm tiny and Alexis Denisof is this enormous bloke.'

They're almost ready in the office set now, with arc lights pouring their radiance through the windows of the set to simulate early-morning

> '**It's very difficult doing authentic fight scenes, because your natural reaction is to try and miss.**'

sunshine. Metin Huseyin, the director of this particular episode, is taking great care over the exact appearance of the office. Each of the directors that Emilia has worked with so far – Mark Mylod, Rachel Talalay, Charlie Higson, Steve Bendelack, Metin Huseyin – has brought a different set of strengths and a different way of doing things to the series, and Emilia values that variety.

'It was an excellent way to do it because each one put their own unique stamp onto their respective episodes, and it gave them a break from what was a pretty gruelling schedule. Mark's just a joy to work with – he's a very smart and talented director. Rachel was also wonderful, and her experience in the special-effects industry brought a real filmic quality to hers.' Emilia watches as Bob Mortimer walks over towards the set. 'Also,' she adds with a smile, 'because Rachel and I had never worked with any of this lot before, we were in a similar position and were able to stick together when we couldn't understand all the in-jokes.'

The core of the series is, of course, the love-triangle between Jeff, Jeannie and Marty, and one of the big unanswered questions is how Jeannie and Marty ever got together in the first place. Emilia has a theory that it all centres on the restaurant where we see her working in 'Drop Dead'.

'He probably came in to eat there with Jeff and she instantly fancied him. I like to think Marty suddenly came into her life and changed it

irrevocably. His "off-the-wall-ness" was probably something she latched on to straight away.'

That 'latching on to' was something that happened in real life as well.

'Vic and I saw each other for a few months during the shoot,' Emilia admits, 'and it was terrific fun. Hopefully that shines through in the series. I'm sure the fact that we were seeing each other helped with a bit of that on-screen chemistry. And why not? We were having a great time.'

Someone arrives to call Emilia Fox for the next shot, in which she and Bob Mortimer have to discuss plastic bags and self-defence lessons. Bogged down in the intricate detail of lines, shots and scenes, it must be difficult to get any kind of overview of the series as a whole, but she is in no doubt about why it succeeds.

'There's a real vacuum for this kind of stuff,' she says. 'Television schedules seem to be full of fly-on-the-wall documentaries and decorating shows. Charlie's spot-on when he says there's a need for something more escapist, something that works as both a drama and as a gentle comedy. It's a great mix. And the show's got so many layers, and a combination of so many different factors, that it stands the test of being watched over and over. It's a real achievement.'

Which means, presumably, that she would be happy to keep going as Jeannie Hurst if there is a third series.

As she moves away, she glances down at the sharply cut dress she's wearing: just one of the many sets of stylish clothes she wears in the series. 'I can't wait to get back into Jeannie's shoes,' she says wistfully. 'Especially if I'm allowed to keep them this time.'

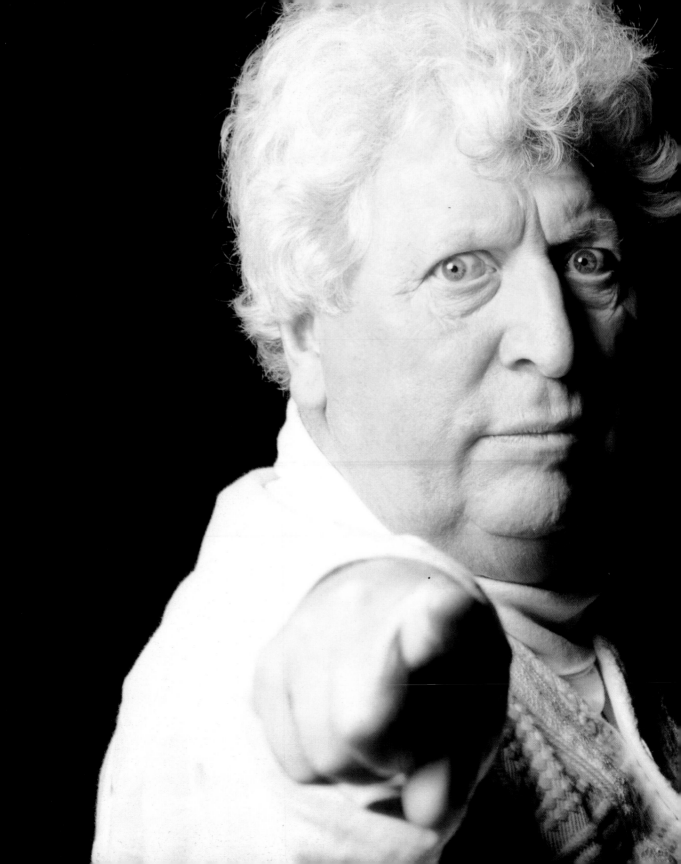

'my mortality has been put on hold'

an audience with tom baker

'I used to want to be liked,' says Tom Baker reflectively, as he sits back in a comfortable chair in the smoky atmosphere of his local pub. 'Then the older I got, I wanted to be loved. Now, in the twilight of my years, I'm really into being adored unconditionally.'

There seems precious little chance of audiences not adoring Tom Baker. In real life he was a trainee monk and a bricklayer before becoming an actor, while in the fantasy world of film and television he has given us memorable performances as, amongst many other characters, Rasputin the Mad Monk, a zombie artist and Sherlock Holmes. His roles as two separate doctors have, however, provided him with instant household recognition. In the early 1990s he became an unusual heart-throb as the eccentric surgeon Professor Hoyt in the popular television series *Medics*, but it is his seven years in the long-running series *Doctor Who*, playing an alien hero who travels through time and space in a machine known as the

TARDIS, that still makes people stop him in the street. And which led, incidentally, to Charlie Higson's request that he play Wyvern in the new *Randall & Hopkirk (Deceased)* series.

'I love still being known as the Doctor,' says Baker. 'It really is an enormous privilege to be recognized by fans of the show all these years on and there's no point trying to resist it. They did a *This Is Your Life* on me a while ago and after it was broadcast I was in the supermarket doing some shopping when a young lady with two small children saw me and sent them running up to ask if I was the Doctor. I'm the only man in the entire kingdom to whom the children's advice "Don't talk to strangers" simply doesn't apply. That's a wonderful feeling, it really is. They created me, I belong to them.'

As he glances around the pub, Baker is only too well aware of the power that his position confers on him with his fans – a power which he draws on in his role as Wyvern as well.

'Sometimes,' he admits, 'you can see my appearance for them has triggered off some desperate fantasy which we mutually indulge ourselves in. I see beggars and the sort in the street, and I'll go to give them a few quid and we both know what's expected. Here they are, wretched and cold, selling the *Big Issue*, and when they see me I'm the Doctor, with a plan of salvation. I'll say to them, "Meet me in St Peter's Square at nine o'clock, put the word out," and by the time evening has come around, this beggar and his friends are milling around the square in their hundreds. Then I materialize in the TARDIS and they all squeeze on board. Of course, there's always one who's late, and so he runs through the square just as the TARDIS dematerializes and I'm whisking off all his friends to some better place. There's great confusion as everyone asks "Where have all the beggars gone?" and this poor chap has to try and tell them they all went into a police box and disappeared. But the poor fellow's deranged so no-one believes him.'

Television doesn't often provide heroes for us to look up to – more often it gives us tormented or confused characters with whom we are meant to identify – but in the Doctor, and also in Wyvern, Tom Baker has created someone all-knowing, avuncular and yet dangerous enough to be interesting: the perfect role model.

'To be a children's hero, certainly through the informality of the medium of television, means that by default you become a family hero,' he points out. 'And family heroes have much more longevity than others. But *Doctor Who* was always a predominantly British phenomenon, and you have also to understand the psyche of the British people. We're a terribly complicated lot. We seek out the most unlikely heroes. I'm an enormous fan of people like Des O'Connor and Michael Barrymore because, very cleverly and self-knowingly, they've created a certain persona

'I used to want to be liked. Then the older I got, I wanted to be loved. Now, in the twilight of my years, I'm really into being adored unconditionally.'

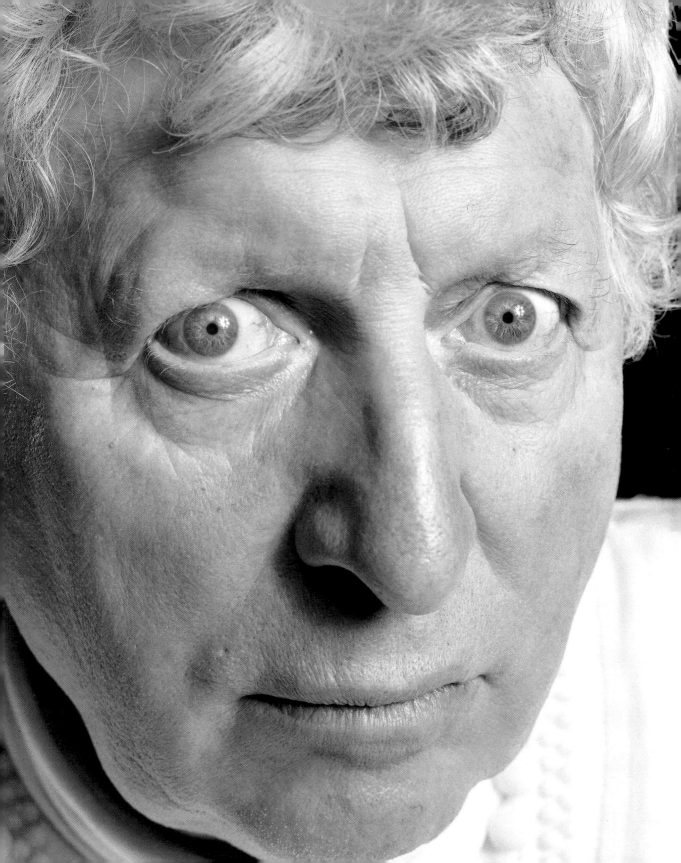

which families respond to. They've made themselves into heroes by being very quirky, reinventing a style of old-fashioned entertainment that people love.'

And it's a standing that means he will be remembered for a long time to come.

He agrees. 'You have to be familiar with death to understand the phenomenon. What doesn't occur to young people is that all moving pictures, especially with sound, confer a kind of immortality on to mortal actors like myself. To me, my heroes like Cary Grant and Humphrey Bogart aren't dead. I never knew Cary Grant, but I know of him because of his movies. All the things we adore about him are there for all to see, preserved for ever on celluloid. I feel I've cheated death in a way – my mortality has been put on hold because of this wonderful iconic status my role as the Doctor has given me. And the strange thing is it's all rather accidental. I mean I've co-operated with it, of course, but I'm still the Doctor wherever I go in the world. I can never be anything else.'

But of course he can. Now he can be Wyvern: a character whose mortality has truly been put on hold. Charlie Higson grew up watching Tom Baker's portrayal of the Doctor, and when he created Wyvern for *Randall & Hopkirk (Deceased)* he knew exactly who he wanted – someone who could be distant and yet caring, magisterial and yet whimsical. Tom Baker was the only choice of actor for the part.

'One of the wonderful things about my situation is that, in the closing days of my life, people like Charlie are now in executive positions of power and they're licensed to some extent to say, "Oh, we'll get Tom in because we used to watch him when we were young." Charlie never asked to see me, he just made a straight offer and of course I accepted, after we'd all had this jolly meal together. He claimed I was the first thought for Wyvern, which was awfully nice of him.'

Baker is, of course, under no illusions about why he was really offered the role. 'Charlie didn't

'People say they're not actors and I say rubbish, they're more important than that. They're stars.'

know me, but he knew the Doctor, and that's what he wanted. It's a very nice feeling, one of great benevolence when people say "We'll get Tom in" when in fact they mean they'll get the Doctor in. That's what they mean in their imaginations. They're inviting a version of the Doctor.'

Despite his immense experience, and of course his magisterial qualities, Tom Baker is quick to pay tribute to the man who cast him. 'The thing with Charlie,' he says, 'is that he's an immensely talented man, very humbling really. He's written all these books and performed and written all these wonderful comedic roles. He has this bumbling humility and a gentle comic way of

'I'm the only man in the entire kingdom
to whom the children's advice "don't
talk to strangers" simply doesn't apply.'

*Right: Tom Baker's magisterial,
yet eccentric, presence made
him the only choice for the part
of Marty's mentor, Wyvern.*
Below: *Vic Reeves shares a
'blue screen moment' with
Tom Baker and Matt Lucas.
Watching closely in the
background are Vic and Bob's
stand-ins, David Oliver and
Brian Tonks.*

approving everything you do without feeling you've been tested.'

Having chosen his perfect Wyvern, Charlie Higson wisely left the skilled actor to get on with the job. 'He'd already bought into this sort of broad, coarse style I have,' Baker says, self-effacingly. 'He just left me to my own devices. Actually, he did pop into my caravan and supervise the costume people adorning me in this ridiculously flouncy outfit with pearls and big flappy bits. Then he saw me going over the top, smiled and walked off. I mean, there are no rules, are there? How do you play a ghost? How do the dead behave? No-one knows. It's a perfect role really. The only letters of complaint I can imagine I'll get will be from disaffected spiritualists.'

In most series in which Tom Baker has played a leading role he has been allowed to wander around interacting with all kinds of other people, be he saving the universe as the Doctor or merely saving the odd life as Professor Hoyt. In *Randall & Hopkirk*, however, he only gets to talk to Vic Reeves while standing in front of a blue screen. Dealing with a man known more for his anarchic comedy than his acting experience has not, however, caused Baker any heartache.

'I got on terribly well with Vic,' he laughs. 'The thing is, people say they're not actors and I say rubbish, they're more important than that. They're stars. There's a difference. This technique of being a competent or glib actor is not at all the same as simply existing in a state of stardom. The distinction is that stars, unlike actors, have a kind of personality that in itself appeals to the public imagination and that's how they build up this huge reservoir of affection. True stardom is such an elusive quality. If we knew what it was we'd manufacture it.'

Fortunately Tom Baker, actor, had no problems working alongside Vic Reeves, star.

'Because he's a star, rather than an actor, it was rather like messing around with a rather highly strung dog. He watches you all the time and he's very quick on the uptake.'

Baker pauses and sips at his drink, reflecting on the differences between actors and stars, aware of the fact that the real Tom Baker is hidden behind the roles he has played, whereas the roles played by Vic Reeves hide behind the man.

'When people come and see me on the tours I do, they don't come to see me, Tom Baker. Of course they don't – they don't know me. But they know the Doctor and that's what they want to see. Heroes of the film and television – particularly television because it implants these personalities into a domestic context – have the ability to catapult you back into your own childhood. That's what the Doctor does for so many people. I can take them back to happy times, watching the television on a Saturday night, the football results, *Basil Brush*, *The Two Ronnies* and *The Generation Game*.'

It's certainly true – ask the woman and her children in the supermarket, ask the beggars who sell the *Big Issue* on the street. Tom Baker is like a member of the family, a slightly eccentric uncle who dispenses sweets and odd advice in equal measure.

Tom Baker pauses, reflecting on what he said earlier about wanting to be liked when he was young, wanting to be loved when he got older, and, in the twilight of his years, wanting to be unconditionally adored.

'Charlie,' he says, with magisterial finality, 'caught me at a time when I was getting worried that I might not even be liked.'

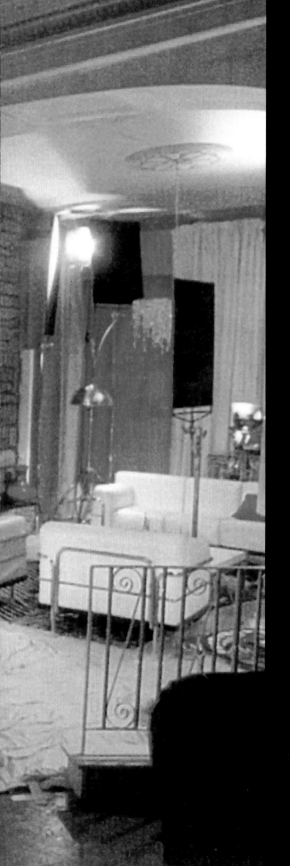

preparing the ingredients

pre-production activity

Filming isn't something that can be made up on the spur of the moment, like performance art or improv theatre. A director can't just turn up somewhere nice, switch the camera on and hope that he or she can capture a classy performance from an unrehearsed performer. Even assuming a script already exists and doesn't need rewriting, locations have to be found, sets have to be constructed and costumes have to be designed and made. Like going to war, success lies in meticulous planning...

Storyboards

Storyboards are normally something one associates with big-budget Hollywood movies. Drawn up at an early stage of production, they act as a translation between the written word of the script and the visual medium of the screen, enabling everyone concerned to break down something like '*A car chase ensues*' into a sequence of shots that tell with minimum confusion how the chase spreads out over several minutes. Similar to a comic strip, it presents the narrative in a series of linked frames.

It's rare for television programmes to need storyboards – they don't usually have enough complicated action to make them necessary, even if they have enough time and money to pay for them. *Randall & Hopkirk (Deceased)* is different. With something like five hundred effects shots in the first series alone, Producer Charlie Higson and Executive Producer Simon Wright felt the need to have something that everyone could use as the basis for their work – a collective imagination that everyone had immediate access to.

Mike Nicholson, the storyboard artist, had done similar work in television advertising for many years, and had previously worked with Charlie on the Channel 4 film show *Kiss Kiss Bang Bang*, for which he had provided some short

Ext. - Crossroads - Day:

Top-shot as Bechard spins into pit.

movie-themed animated sequences. More recently he worked on the title sequence for the new BBC comedy series *World of Pub*.

'All directors are different,' Charlie Higson points out: 'some have a very visual sense, some are excellent at drawing, some can't draw to save their lives but know exactly what they want, some can only work out what they want when they're physically there on location and some are just insane. It's the job of the poor storyboard artist to somehow divine what it is the director wants to achieve and get it down on paper so that everybody else involved has some idea what the thing's going to look like – and then the director changes it all on the day.'

'Mark Mylod liked to provide his own detailed storyboard roughs,' Mike remembers. 'Rachel Talalay tended to sketch and discuss ideas during meetings, while Charlie occasionally acted out the more physical bits of business – notably Marty's song-and-dance number.'

Mike's work on series two of the show closely paralleled his experiences on series one, although he was working largely with different directors.

Above and opposite right: Mike Nicholson's storyboards show the key visual components of the scene (in this case, the destruction of Hadell Wroxted at the end of 'A Man of Substance') and also convey a real sense of movement, speed and energy. *Opposite far right:* ideas for demons to populate the Afterlife.

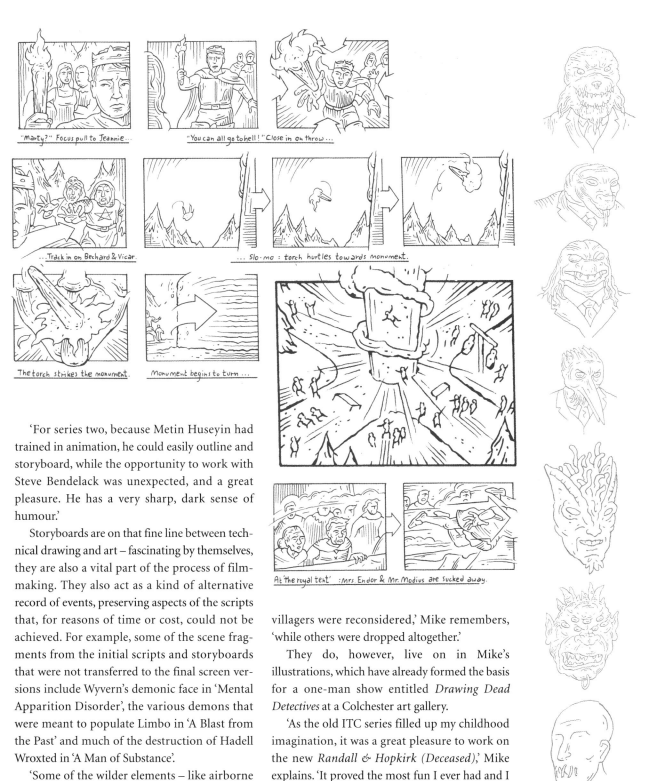

"Marty?" Focus pull to Jeannie...

"You can all go to hell!" Close in on throw...

...Track in on Bechard & Vicar.

... Slo-mo : torch hurtles towards monument.

The torch strikes the monument.

Monument begins to turn ...

At 'the royal tent' : Mrs. Endor & Mr. Modius are sucked away.

'For series two, because Metin Huseyin had trained in animation, he could easily outline and storyboard, while the opportunity to work with Steve Bendelack was unexpected, and a great pleasure. He has a very sharp, dark sense of humour.'

Storyboards are on that fine line between technical drawing and art – fascinating by themselves, they are also a vital part of the process of filmmaking. They also act as a kind of alternative record of events, preserving aspects of the scripts that, for reasons of time or cost, could not be achieved. For example, some of the scene fragments from the initial scripts and storyboards that were not transferred to the final screen versions include Wyvern's demonic face in 'Mental Apparition Disorder', the various demons that were meant to populate Limbo in 'A Blast from the Past' and much of the destruction of Hadell Wroxted in 'A Man of Substance'.

'Some of the wilder elements – like airborne props and bodies, fiery hell-pits and exploding villagers were reconsidered,' Mike remembers, 'while others were dropped altogether.'

They do, however, live on in Mike's illustrations, which have already formed the basis for a one-man show entitled *Drawing Dead Detectives* at a Colchester art gallery.

'As the old ITC series filled up my childhood imagination, it was a great pleasure to work on the new *Randall & Hopkirk (Deceased)*,' Mike explains. 'It proved the most fun I ever had and I got paid for it!'

An introduction to production design

'The production designer's job,' says Grenville Horner, who filled the position on the first series, 'is to realize the visualization of the script and try to give it a fully rounded, three-dimensional aspect. That means taking overall charge of every element of the production – from sets and lighting to costumes and locations.'

One has to start somewhere with a job that big, and it would have been tempting to look at the original series to see where the new series had come from, but Grenville deliberately avoided that option.

'The first thing I did was to make sure I didn't watch any of the originals,' he says. 'It's very easy to get your vision compromised by baggage like that, so I studiously avoided taking home any of the ITC video cassettes.'

Grenville wasn't available for the second series of *Randall & Hopkirk (Deceased)* and, with many

> 'A designer's job is reading a script and solving all the visual problems. If you have a feature budget, you can build everything, but we haven't got the money so we have to find locations.'
> Simon Waters

of the major elements already in place (the office, Wyvern's room, Marty's wardrobe), Simon Waters was brought on board. With something like six hundred commercials to his credit, Simon knew how to solve problems quickly, but as he himself admits, 'This is the first thing I've done in television for twenty years.'

'I look at a designer's job as reading a script and solving all the visual problems,' he says. 'If you had a feature budget, straight away you know you could build everything, but we know we haven't got the money so we're stuck with having to find locations. The first job is finding the locations.' He shrugs. 'You've got a pot of money and you're constantly balancing what to do with that money.'

Like many of the people who have worked on the series, Simon feels that there is very little else out there that offers the same scope and variety.

'That's what attracted me to this project,' he enthuses. 'It's such a fantastic opportunity for a designer because it's so bizarre. There's very little on television that pushes the boat out like this programme does – not only with the design but the whole concept and the way it's shot.'

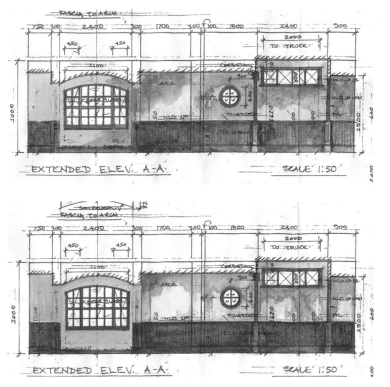

EXTENDED ELEV. A-A.   SCALE 1:50

EXTENDED ELEV. A-A.   SCALE 1:50

Production design – the office set

There are only two sets that turn up again and again in *Randall & Hopkirk (Deceased)* – the firm's office and Wyvern's room. And only one of those sets is real.

Wyvern's rooms were created entirely within the virtual memory of a computer, but the firm's offices are constructed from the traditional tools of the trade – hardboard, paint and gaffer tape.

Grenville Horner was the man who dreamed up the office set. Instead of looking to the Seventies original for an overall style, Horner turned the clock back further, and took his inspiration instead from 1940s film noir.

'I wanted this sort of American PI feel to it,' he says, 'a sort of old-fashioned UK version. We went for this partition wall with frosted glass and it worked great… I imagined two blokes sharing an office and how, over time, they'd each territorialize their space. Each desk would accumulate the stuff that people collect: their pictures and their books and their games and their junk. And of course, one of these characters dies at the very outset, so I wanted Marty's desk to remain as it was, whilst Jeff's continued to change. Marty's half of the office would freeze, like some odd little shrine, with neither Jeannie nor Jeff having the heart to clear it away.'

The set itself is a marvel. Rather dull and tawdry between takes, it suddenly glows a surprising amber when the huge lighting rigs are aimed at it.

'It's quite stylized,' Grenville points out, 'but since this room is the pivot for each of the stories, I wanted it to be as real as possible. That meant putting in immense amounts of detail which – quite frankly – the viewer was never, ever going to see. But I always think overdoing the particulars in such a central scene like this helps everyone immerse themselves in the story, from the directors to the actors.'

Too small to be picked up by the camera lens, the 'detail' is the kind of thing that's only apparent if you're in the set itself. Sitting at Jeff's desk and turning the papers over in your hands, or running your eyes across a notice-board, it's hard not to believe that you're in a real office, rather than a wooden box constructed inside a sound stage.

Grenville laughs. 'It was silly really. I mean, we had letter-headed paper with the full address of the agency, business cards, envelopes written to their address… It was incredibly detailed. But I think the room came alive because of that detail, even if you can't see it on screen.'

For series two, new Production Designer Simon Waters made some changes to Grenville's original design.

'I made it a lot busier and a lot scruffier,' he reveals. 'That was the whole point – the pair of them were threadbare and hadn't got any dosh, and I didn't think that it came across. The colours were quite bright, so I made it a lot more subdued.'

One of the things that has remained constant between series one and series two is the large window, the dominant feature of the office. The blue sky and rooftops that appear so convincing on screen are painted on a fake brick wall a few feet from the fake window. And yet, even this is part of the plan – in fact, it's a deliberate reference on Charlie Higson's part to the tawdriness of the backdrops in the original series.

'Is that a picture?' Gordon Stylus asks Jeff and Marty in 'Drop Dead', the first episode of the series, as he glances out.

'Yeah, it was just a blank wall out there before,' Jeff replies. 'We thought it would cheer the place up a bit.'

'It's not very good,' Stylus – the world's worst artist – sneers.

The office of Randall & Hopkirk (Deceased) was inspired by a stylized 1940s Philip Marlowe look. But it was another example of combining established styles with modern sensibilities to achieve an almost timeless archetype.

Production design – the jungle set

Anger's large office has been almost totally converted into an Amazonian jungle. There is a hothouse atmosphere; heat haze and insects buzzing about.

A few simple lines in Gareth Roberts's script for 'Pain Killers', but a major headache for an art director who is balancing the many and various requirements of an entire series against a limited budget. Especially when you consider the casual, almost throwaway description later on: *Jeannie is wandering through the jungle, watering, spraying, poking about. She pushes aside a tree and to her astonishment discovers the wreckage of an aeroplane.*

How on Earth does one create an Amazonian jungle with a crashed aeroplane? Within a few days? On a tight budget?

'Jungle plants cost an absolute fortune,' Simon Waters, points out, 'so you think, "How can we create a South American jungle relatively inexpensively?" Rather than go through a greenery company, I went straight to the Forestry Commission.'

Their suggestion was to use real trees from a forest near Farnham in Surrey. The trees were being felled anyway, as part of the normal forest management process, so why not use them?

According to Simon, 'Cutting those trees down doesn't cost anything. It's the transport that costs. We got a hundred and twenty trees. I chose ones with very straight trunks and without any greenery on. Then we used creepers to create the impression of a tropical rain forest. Old Man's Beard, it's called. I hung a load of moss, tied on with wires… A few big banana palms and big leafy plants in the foreground and it creates the illusion.'

Ironically, as well as standing in for the Amazonian jungle, the forest was also used to represent

Latvia in episode six of series two – 'The Glorious Butranekh' – and had previously stood in for Europe in the film *Gladiator*. A well-travelled forest.

Having got the trees out of the way, the aeroplane was the next problem.

'I could have turned round to Charlie and said, "We can't afford it, so you can't have the aeroplane,"' says Simon, 'but that would have been a little bit of a cop-out. Actually the aeroplane was very inexpensive. We went to a big aeroplane-breaker's in Colchester. Transporting it was the main cost.'

As the script makes clear, the jungle office is actually located hundreds of feet beneath the green fields of England. In order to convey this point, Simon had to find a way of placing the set in a rather more futuristic context.

'I said to Charlie, "We should go for a metal floor." That tells you straight away that it's a Bond-type set.'

Opposite: *The convincing atmosphere of an Amazonian forest was helped by the use of real trees and the presence of tiny details – including a lizard in a specimen jar as a prop.*

Above: *Colonel Anger's Jungle Room in 'Pain Killers': first the envisaged surroundings are sketched by the production designer (above) and then constructed to bring the vision alive (top).*

Left and opposite: Simon Waters's designs for the interior of Boyle's Department Store in 'Two Can Play at That Game' owe something to 1960s Pop Art .
Opposite right: Following a certain amount of digital manipulation, Hornsey Town Hall (far right) in London's Crouch End stood in for the exterior of Boyle's Department Store.

seven days a week, and as the bulk of the episode takes place in it we knew we had to do at least five days' filming at this location.'

Finding that kind of spare time in one block was impossible, short of closing down an entire department of a real department store. And the budget just didn't exist for that.

'The only alternative,' Charlie continues, 'is that you find somewhere and you dress it as a department store, at which point you're suddenly up against a massive prop hire fee, plus all the construction and dressing you've got to do. Obviously if you're in Hollywood you get a huge set and you build the thing, but we have a very small budget for construction. So we were stuck with this difficulty.'

Solving the problem required a shift in perspective: Charlie turned it into a feature.

'As the episode was written as a homage to the old *Avengers* thing of going into this weird environment where you get trapped, we eventually decided to go fully down that route and make it a complete Sixties-style abstract environment where you haven't really got a set, it's just black walls and things suspended. So it's a surreal, psychedelic world that we enter.'

The sets were effectively constructed in the studio, and re-dressed as necessary to give the impression that the cast were moving from department to department.

'I came up with this idea of doing it in a black box,' Production Designer Simon Waters enthuses. 'We put up these big silk walls, and then we created these circles of light, and just did these big painted cut-out legs. Visually, it's quite a theatrical approach: not the sort of thing you get to do on television very often.'

Production design – the Boyle's Department Store set

This part of the store is seriously weird. It's huge and empty – falling away to blackness all around. There is a row of giant stockinged legs stretching away as to infinity. There's an old-fashioned cosmetics stand, with outsize bottles of perfume on it, large and childlike.

The initial intention had been to film the Mark Gatiss and Jeremy Dyson episode, 'Two Can Play at That Game', in an actual department store, re-dressing as necessary to emphasize the surreal nature of the plot. The production team soon realized that would be impossible.

'We came up against a problem which we didn't envisage at the time, and which we didn't think through,' Charlie Higson reveals, 'which was that it's virtually impossible to film in a department store unless you've got a large budget, because (a) there's not very many department stores left, and (b) they're all now open pretty well

'We decided to make it a Sixties-style abstract environment where you haven't really got a set.'
Charlie Higson

Costume design

June Nevin, Costume Designer on all thirteen episodes of *Randall & Hopkirk (Deceased)*, cut her teeth as an assistant on three series of *Jeeves and Wooster*. She previously worked with Vic Reeves and Bob Mortimer on *Shooting Stars*, *Families at War* and *The Smell of Reeves and Mortimer*, which led to them recommending her for their new project, but it was her work on the US television series *Tales from the Crypt* that convinced Charlie Higson and Simon Wright that she could handle the fantasy elements – elements that just aren't present in British television these days.

'It's very seldom you get such a creative job,' she says. 'And there's no money to do it: we're having to make stuff out of cardboard and two bits of sticky-backed plastic. It's *Blue Peter* designing!'

The aim with *Randall & Hopkirk (Deceased)*, lack of money notwithstanding, was to ensure that nothing about the series tied it specifically to a particular 'era'. Like the ITC series it grew out of, the series should still stand up in thirty years' time. One way of doing this was to make the costumes of the main characters deliberately echo classic styles.

'Jeff is always wearing 1960s American suits and a leather jacket,' June says by way of an example. 'And in the first series, Marty's long white coat was based on a painting of Brahms from about 1840. This series we've really snapped him up: late Sixties, early Seventies double-breasted, high-cross jackets and a coat. We were going to be shooting in the winter, and I thought if I put him in jackets and coats and waistcoats it's like layering so he won't be so chilly when we're filming. It's a much cleaner look – I'm really happy with it. And he's got hats.'

With Wyvern, the idea of harking back in time was taken to extremes.

'I said to Charlie, "What I want to do with Wyvern is, I want him to look like he's lived for ever, and he's just picked out various things that he's liked throughout the ages and he wears them willy nilly." He's got a pair of Versace white trousers that he wears with a polo neck, and an eighteenth-century waistcoat, and he might wear the britches with the polo neck, or the britches with a cricket jumper, and he's got white stockings with trainers. It's just a complete mish-mash.'

As with Marty, Wyvern's costume was modi-fied for the second series.

'This series he's got a Cardinal's robe, which is like a fifteenth-century court robe with a cape. And I've given him a crystal, because he said he wanted one. He had beads last year.'

Over the course of thirteen episodes, each of which has different requirements for style and period, it's the one-off costumes that provide June and her team with the greatest challenges.

'It's like doing little feature films,' she says. 'On this last series I've had to design eleventh-century Latvian soldiers, then 1940s costumes, then I had to invent uniforms for a secret lab – every single one was different.'

Particular costumes that stand out in June's mind include Marty's 'King of the World' robes – based on an illustration in the Bayeux Tapestry – and the red siren dress worn by actress Jennifer Calvert (playing Lauren Dee) in the episode 'A Man of Substance'.

'I drew that about five or six weeks before we even started shooting to show Mark Mylod what I wanted – this Lauren Bacall *femme fatale* – and he shot her leaning against the wall, which is exactly how I'd imagined it all those weeks beforehand.'

Strangely, in the time she's been working on the series, the costumes that have caused June the most trouble have been the ones that were, on the surface, the most featureless ones of all – the Pawns in 'Marshall & Snellgrove'.

'I saw the storyboards and I thought, "That looks interesting." The first thing that came into my head when I read the script was those lovely long duster coats in *Once Upon a Time in the*

Above: Sketches for one of the islanders in 'O Happy Isle'.
Left: A 'wood nymph' design from 'A Man of Substance'.
Below left: June Nevin's original illustration for the femme fatale dress from 'A Man of Substance' was picked up as a directorial element by Mark Mylod.
Opposite: June Nevin based Marty's 'King of the World' costume in 'A Man of Substance' on elements from the Bayeux Tapestry.

West. I thought if we could get that sort of shape going, with the round heads…' She sighs. 'They were a horrendous problem. The actors were young girls, about five-foot tall, and they had to be able to see out of the headpieces. You can do miracles with all sorts of colours, but white is impossible because the pigments are so dense. In the end we put a tiny eye-line across the head bowl and then covered it with a bit of net.'

That may have been the biggest challenge, but the biggest problem was something much simpler – the sheer number of costumes that had to be made. Especially when a character died and turned up in Limbo.

'Every time somebody dies, the thing that they died in has got to be copied into white. I said to Charlie at one point, "Will you please stop killing men off, because it's cheaper to make women's white clothes than it is to make men's." Your basic suit is five hundred and fifty quid and then you've got to pay for the fabric on top of that, and you've got to have three of them because, even if it's a small part, coffee might get spilled, or there might be a stunt double who needs one, or something.'

It's always the small things that cause the most annoyance…

Above: Mrs Glauneck
(Elizabeth Spriggs) and the
wood nymphs from 'A Man of
Substance'.
Left: Mrs Glauneck's alter ego,
Lauren Dee (Jennifer Calvert),
in 'A Man of Substance'.
Below: Another islander
costume from 'O Happy Isle'.
June Nevin designed the
costumes around local activities
– farming, hunting and fishing.
Opposite: Marty as the 'King of
the World' and also, apparently,
as Toulouse Lautrec.

preparing the ingredients

Jeannie's look

June Nevin had strong opinions on the way Jeannie should be dressed. Like all the other main characters her style contains many references to classic styles that won't date, but in her case the references are to a person rather than an era.

'The whole thing about Jeannie is that I wanted her to be more of an Audrey Hepburn than a Diana Rigg. She never carries a handbag: we decided it was the sort of thing Jeannie wouldn't do. She always wears gloves. She's always got little heels on. It's that kind of tiny classic things. Even though she's doing her kung fu she should always look marvellous and untouchable.'

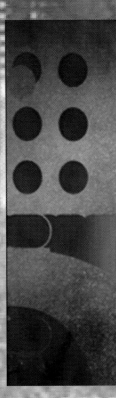

The title sequence

Think of *The Persuaders*, those solid, definitive, echoing piano chords leading into a fuzzy bass line, courtesy of John Barry, all accompanying the life story of the show's heroes as illustrated by a montage of photographs and headlines. Think of *The Prisoner*, Ron Grainer's soaring trumpet line and twanging guitar set against a miniature movie telling of how Number Six is 'retired' to the village. Think of *The Professionals*, a thundering brass section and a twanging guitar bursting your speakers as an executive car drives through a plate-glass window.

Title sequences. They don't make them like that any more.

Except that they do. For *Randall & Hopkirk (Deceased)*, Simon Wright and Charlie Higson wanted to recapture the feel of those old series with something that was modern and yet timeless, Bond-like and yet original.

A tall order? Perhaps, but it worked. Firstly, David Arnold and Tim Simenon's theme tune instantly worms its way into your mind and takes up residence, just as Arnold's theme songs for the James Bond films *Tomorrow Never Dies* and *The World is Not Enough* did. Starting with a simple piano riff, it then develops into a lush string-led tune punctuated with brass 'stings'. 'Nice,' as they say on *The Fast Show*.

'Right up front we wanted a theme tune that was as big as the series,' says Simon Wright, 'because the series is very big – each episode it's almost like a large movie in microcosm. So we were looking for something big and something

that really paid homage, not necessarily to *Randall & Hopkirk (Deceased)* but to the Seventies. David Arnold in many respects represents, in his approach to music, everything we wanted. Charlie is a massive fan of David Arnold, although I didn't really know very much about him. But he had a tune that he'd already written, and Charlie brought it back and played it, and we just thought "Wow".'

'Charlie wrote me a letter saying, "Vic and Bob are doing *Randall & Hopkirk (Deceased)* and I'm directing – would you be interested?"' reveals David Arnold, 'and I said, "Of course I would." I've been a big fan of all three of them, ever since I was absolutely nothing and living in a dump. I'm always interested in doing things that sound intriguing, and I knew the original series, although I couldn't remember the theme for it – it didn't strike me as being one of those classics like *The Persuaders* or *The Avengers*.'

Given the short time-scales that apply within television – time-scales that often mean the end of a series is being edited even as the first episodes are being transmitted – David Arnold didn't have the luxury of knowing anything more than 'Vic and Bob are doing *Randall & Hopkirk (Deceased)*.'

'I wrote the thing based on the basic idea,' he says. 'I hadn't seen a script, I hadn't seen any footage, I didn't know what it was going to look like or anything. I did know there was a fantastical element, which meant I could be a little bit outrageous with the music. I didn't have to be period: actually I could be quite camp and exotic. It was all of those ideas together that made me

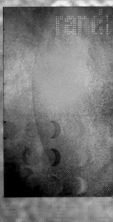

tom baker

think it was something I wanted to do.'

As often happens with David Arnold, the theme wasn't generated from thin air for the series, but was based on something he had already been working on with Tim Simenon.

'I walked in on Tim once when he had a rhythm track going, and I sat down at a keyboard and wrote the melody and chords over the top of his rhythm track. We were always trying to find the right kind of thing to help us finish it off… We tried a couple of different versions just between ourselves – Skin from Skunk Anansie did a vocal on it at one stage, but it was really kinda weird and 'out there'. But I knew the germs of it were good. Sometimes these things come to you and you have to find an outlet for them.'

'The first version I played Charlie was a bit more laid back than the one we finally used, and he said the magic words that everyone says to me – "Can we have it a bit more Bond-y?" I should just get a T-shirt made saying, "Would you like it a bit more Bond-y?"'.

Simon Wright, for one, is glad they did ask David Arnold, if only because what could have been a budget-sapping exercise turned into something magical.

'David Arnold did it for us for free,' Simon says, amazed. 'He's never taken a penny. He simply wrote it and produced it for us. I can't speak highly enough about him.'

'I did it for nothing,' David confirms. 'They had a limited budget and the important thing for me was what people get to hear, so whatever money we had we spent on the recording. We got a great recording, and a great mix, and a great tune. That's what people are going to hear, not whether or not I managed to trouser a thousand quid. Working on big movies means that I can afford to do things like that.'

While the Arnold/Simenon theme tune weaves its magic spell, the titles and credits appear, ghost-like, against a background designed by Graham Woods at graphics company Tomato. Golden bubbles weave past each other on a black background, elegant, sophisticated and yet enticing.

'We wanted to pay homage to the Seventies,' Simon Wright adds, 'and they came up with the bare bones of it very quickly. It has all the flickering flames and the semi-homage to the Bond movies we wanted. I love it.'

Title sequences are sometimes a signal for people to get up, talk and make a cup of tea. In this case, it would be like walking past the Mona Lisa to get to an ice-cream van.

baking the cake

filming the episodes

The moment the camera starts rolling is the culmination of a massive amount of activity. Hundreds of people have done their jobs in ensuring that the various parts of the jigsaw puzzle have come together. Now it's up to the actors.

The glassy eye of the camera is pointed straight at them. Sound operators, lighting experts, continuity and make-up people, all hold their breath, watching and waiting. This is the sharp end. Before and after this moment there is room for experimentation, for error, for doing it again until it's right. Here, now, as the film whirrs through the camera and the director shouts 'Action!', everything depends on them...

Above: *Director of photography John Ignatius (far right) with Charlie Higson (second from left) and sfx supervisor Charlie Noble (far left) supervises a blue-screen shot involving Vic Reeves as Marty and Matt Lucas as Nesbit.*
Opposite right: *Vic Reeves and Bob Mortimer take a cigarette break during the filming of 'The Best Years of Your Death'.*
Opposite bottom: *Marty and Nesbit prepare to haunt the dreams of Jeff Randall in 'Revenge of the Bog People'.*

What happens on set

Ealing Studios, London – one of the many facilities that Working Title have used for filming the series over the past few years. Somewhere in this maze of buildings George Formby once leaned on a lamppost, strumming his ukulele. Somewhere around here, Alec Guinness donned cassocks, uniforms, dresses and wigs for *Kind Hearts and Coronets*. Just around a corner there's a bar where, who knows, Gracie Fields may even have knocked back the odd half of milk stout.

Today, in one of the massive soundstages – all crumbling brickwork and peeling paint from the outside, all cables and gantries and struts on the inside – elements of two different episodes are being filmed. One side of the interior has been covered with blue sheeting which, thanks to the magic of special effects, will later be replaced with Wyvern's room. Away from the eye-bending mass of blue sits a rough wooden box, about the size of a scout hut, which, incredibly, contains the entire office set. Most importantly of all, sitting to

one side is a folding table with two huge vats of tea and coffee – the essential supplies for any television or film project.

In the office, Bob Mortimer and Emilia Fox are going through their lines for a scene from 'Marshall & Snellgrove', in which a chance remark from Jeannie helps Jeff to unravel the whole mystery. The camera is tucked away to one side. The director, Metin Huseyin, signals he is ready for a take and suddenly the lights are turned up to their full intensity. Bob and Emilia repeat their lines again, and again, until the director is happy.

Everything is suddenly on the move. Bob and Emilia vanish off to their dressing rooms while people lug lights, sound rigs and cables over to the blue sheeting. An ornate chair and a table and chessboard that were resting off to one side are now carried into the centre of the blue sheet. Pieces are carefully placed on the board according to a mysterious plan held by one of the props men. A large camera crane is pushed over so that Metin can capture a shot that starts with the camera looking down at a chess piece, continues with the camera lifting away toward the ceiling and then swooping down until it is looking across the chessboard rather than down on it, then finishes on a slow track toward Tom Baker as he leans forward, picks the chess piece up and holds it in front of his face. It takes an hour and a half to get right. Either the camera isn't lined up on the chess piece at the beginning, or the swoop down ends up in the wrong place, or the crane wobbles as it tracks in. At one point the actor rolls his eyes up to the distant lighting gantries. 'Wouldn't it be easier if I was playing Buckaroo?' he asks, rhetorically.

Finally, when the shot is complete, Vic Reeves bounds on set. He, like Baker, is entirely dressed in white. The chairs and table are removed and the two of them stand there on the blue sheets like strangely shaped clouds floating across a blue sky.

Metin is now moving on to a shot for 'O Happy Isle'. Here Marty has to try and convince Wyvern that he isn't jealous of Jeff any more, but in his enthusiasm things get out of control and Wyvern's room shatters around them. The 'things' will be added later, and for now Reeves and Baker have to mime their panicked reaction to imagined catastrophe. They grimace, duck and flail their arms around for several seconds until Metin tells them to stop.

'Was that too naturalistic?' Baker asks with avuncular concern.

Playing with fire – physical effects

One of the most dramatic, and yet at the same time one of the most artistic, moments of the series occurs at the climax of 'The Best Years of Your Death'. Harriet Banks-Smith, head matron of Radlands School and, incidentally, ringleader of a murderous gang of boys, accidentally sets light to herself and stumbles ablaze down the central aisle of the chapel in a slow-motion ballet of fire.

Despite the sheer artistry of the sequence, it was the practical work of stunt co-ordinator Rod Woodruff that ensured a perfect take and no casualties. 'You can't get complacent with fire,' Woodruff points out. 'No matter how much you plan beforehand, it can still prove unpredictable on the day. That's why it's essential to have back-up, after back-up, after back-up.'

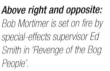
For this sequence, Woodruff was eager to get as long a shot as possible, with the camera tracking the character's stumbling advance down the central aisle, swinging the school's ceremonial sword before her.

'I was looking to stretch the entire sequence out to 25 or 30 seconds,' he says. 'I only wanted to do the stunt once, so the longer it lasted the better. But that's a really long time to be on fire and you have to plan meticulously to ensure everyone's safety.'

In the case of this particular stunt, Rod was not only the co-ordinator, but also the stuntman. That meant having complete control over the sequence, as well as being able to help the director in getting the camera angles right. Once all the positions and timings were established, and once Woodruff was enrobed in three layers of fire-retardant material, as well as in the costume required for the scene, it was time to get the dangerous materials out.

'We use a highly flammable special-effects gel called isopropanol,' he says. 'It's volatile stuff and you have to be very careful where you use it. It'll stick to anything, and it ignites spectacularly.'

Woodruff was smothered in the gel, got to his position at the altar, and then watched as a trail of the gel was laid out down the centre of the aisle. But just before the cameras rolled and the gel ignited, he had an idea.

'I suddenly thought how much better it would look if the sword was on fire as well. It was just an afterthought, so I stopped the action and had a

quick chat with Mark [Mylod]. He was a bit dubious at first – rightly worried it might be too dangerous, I suppose – but in the end we decided it was a go-er. So we gelled up the sword, lit the fuse, and away I went. Looking at the footage now I'm really glad we did it. The sword looks quite spectacular and I think it really made the shot.'

Setting fire to a stuntman is easy. It's putting him out again which is the important bit. This is where Woodruff's meticulous planning and years of experience comes into play.

'You can get quite astonishingly hot in thirty seconds,' he says with admirable calmness. 'I don't take any chances on a stunt like this – or indeed any of my stunts – so during this sequence I had four separate back-up systems. Each one is controlled, so if I get into trouble or things just aren't going right, I have a pre-defined set of movements or gestures which tell any one of the four back-ups to put me out. We all know exactly what the other is doing and with that number of separate supports you can be sure of an immediate, reliable response if needed. But you've got to remember I'm a stuntman – my job is to get the shot the director wants – so I always strive to get the shot finished.'

The shot was enormously successful, but by the end of the thirty seconds Woodruff was in desperate need of being put out. 'In a fire stunt the first priority is killing the fire, and we do that by dousing it in CO_2.' The fire, however, is only half the

problem. 'You've then got to deal with the heat that's still deep within the fabric of the clothing, and it's a heat that'll keep moving in unless you stop it. That means once the fire is out, I direct another back-up to hit any hot-spots with water. Again, it's very control-led so we all know exactly what to do if it gets out of hand.'

And if it does get out of hand?

'There's a team of paramedics standing by,' Woodruff says in the calm tone of voice other men use when discussing five-a-side football or lawn-mowing. 'We all hope they end up with nothing to do.'

Knocking down walls – mechanical effects

There's a moment in 'Paranoia' when the hotel bed containing a naked and handcuffed Jeff Randall is pulled through a wall, courtesy of Marty Hopkirk's spiritual powers, and knocks a villain unconscious. It's tempting to assume that this, like many of the other effects in the series, was created using computers, but it wasn't. All it took was brute force, a fake wall, a lot of compressed air and a couple of men willing to take risks for art. It's called 'mechanical effects', but the anodyne term doesn't do justice to just how physically demanding the process is.

Since most of the action for this episode was filmed in a genuine hotel, and since the director didn't want to ruin a perfectly good hotel room wall, Grenville Horner (series one Production Designer) had to recreate the hotel room on a sound set. This meant duplicating every detail of the room, down to every fixture and fitting.

'What we actually did,' says Grenville, 'was to strip the real hotel room as much as possible. Then we brought in our own props to repopulate it again. For the stunt scene we then took out all of our own stuff and put it into the pretend room. But the devil's in the detail when you do something like this and we had to find out what wallpaper the hotel had used so we could get ours looking exactly the same.'

Once the room was created, it was time to get the machinery in. Central to the stunt was a real bed, strong and sturdy enough to handle being blasted through a wall with stuntman Vincent 'Ginger' Keane attached to it, made up (and dressed down) to resemble Bob Mortimer. The bed was mounted on a pneumatic platform which was programmed to punch it through the wall and collapse it down on top of a second stuntman in a precisely controlled movement.

'It all comes down to planning,' says stunt co-ordinator Rod Woodruff. 'Once the bed was in place, we tested it over and over again, gradually increasing the pressure so it got faster and faster. But we only had two false walls, made out of scored plasterboard, cork bricks and bags of dust.' The stunt, therefore, had to go right second time, if not first. 'Although we'd calculated how much extra force we'd need to break through, it was still something of an unknown. Too little pressure and the bed gets stopped by the wall, too much and you injure the stuntman.'

The stuntman in question, standing in front of the wall, waiting for a bed to come crashing into the small of his back, was Andy Smart. 'I had to stand with my back to the false wall,' Smart recalls, 'and, on a cue, the bed would burst through and hit me. There was a lot of movement in the bed-frame because it had to travel horizontally another four feet or so and then land on top of me so only my head was left poking out. That meant the moment it struck, I had to collapse down and let it move above me before the machinery dropped it down. This all had to take place in less than a second… I'd personally never done a stunt like this before, and neither had any of my colleagues, so we were all very intent on making sure we'd got the preparations right and were ready for any eventuality.'

'It took eight hours to set that shot up,' Woodruff confirms. 'At the end of the day, the director has a vision, and we offer ways of making

Mike Nicholson's storyboards for the scene in 'Paranoia' where Marty accidentally pulls a hotel bed through the wall (below), *and the scene as filmed* (opposite).

it happen. The closer you get to the vision the better, but safety always has to be your number-one priority. That's why something like this can take so long. You can't slam a metal bed into someone's back at 500 lbs per square inch without getting it perfectly choreographed and making sure there's nothing that can go wrong.'

Andy Smart – the man on the wrong end of the bed – could potentially have been in for a protracted period of osteopathy if things went even the slightest bit wrong. The temptation to swathe himself in half a ton of bubble-wrap must have been intense, but he resisted. 'I wanted to be able to feel the bed hit me immediately,' he said. 'Too much padding could have reduced my reflex time and what was critical to this stunt was me getting horizontal as soon as possible.'

No matter how far special-effects technology advances, there are some things that will always require nuts, bolts, spanners, brute force and real people. Ever since the days of Mack Sennett and the Keystone Cops, mechanical effects have been the backbone of the industry, and *Randall & Hopkirk (Deceased)* is no exception.

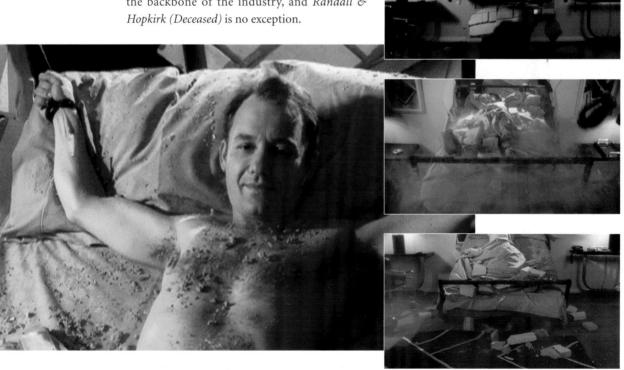

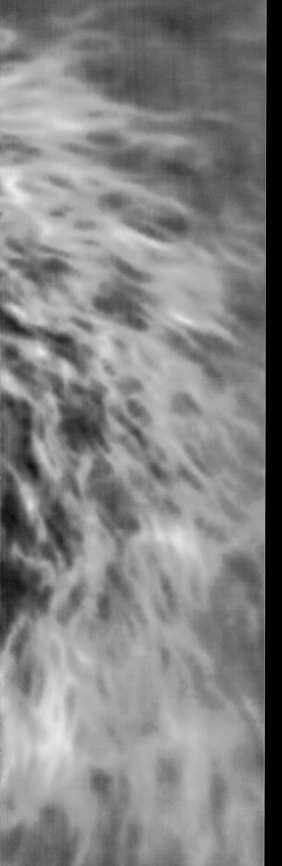

putting the icing on the cake

post-production activity

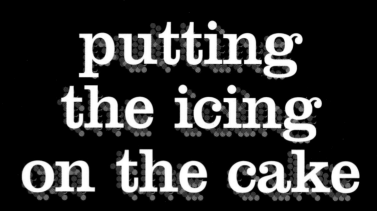

A pile of film cans holding tightly wound spirals of celluloid: the only visible result of all the months of pre-production effort and filming. Now it's time for the editor to select the best scenes, trim them to their ideal length and splice them together. Now it's time for the special-effects technicians to add things that don't really exist. Now it's time for the sound editor to clean up the soundtrack and for the composer to add music, highlighting the drama and the tension. And all this must be done while the clock is ticking, and transmission day is getting closer...

Special Effects – Double Negative

If there is one thing that distinguishes the new *Randall & Hopkirk (Deceased)* from the original – apart, of course, from the snappier scripts and the improved budget – it's the special effects. The original series limited itself to Marty's sudden appearances and the odd shot of him walking through a wall. WTTV were, however, painfully aware that today's audiences would want more. Much more.

Luckily, WTTV share a building with Double Negative, a special-effects company with an impressive pedigree: in the fourteen months prior to the first transmission of *Randall & Hopkirk (Deceased)* they were the talent behind effects scenes in films such as *Pitch Black, Mission: Impossible 2, Nutty Professor II, Whatever Happened to Harold Smith?* and in the innovative fairy story for television *The 10th Kingdom.*

With a top special-effects company literally just across the corridor, WTTV would have been foolish to go anywhere else for their effects. Usually in film and television, special-effects companies are presented with a finished script and asked to help turn it into reality. *Randall & Hopkirk (Deceased)* was different, with Double Negative brought in early on and involved right from the start. During the subsequent writing and re-writing of the scripts, they worked with Charlie Higson to construct scenes in such a way that as much of Working Title's budget as possible ended up on screen.

'In our book there's only two types of special effects,' says Double Negative's co-founder Matthew Holben: 'good ones and bad ones. Good ones are born from meticulous planning and so we threw as much resource as we could into conceptualizing the sequences as a whole, and then breaking each of the scenes down into their individual elements. We had our own ideas, a lot of which were moulded into shape by the production designer and the directors.'

'At that stage I didn't really have a clue what was possible,' Charlie Higson admits. 'Without the multi-million-pound budgets of big Hollywood blockbusters we had to be very aware of what our relatively limited resources could or could not achieve. Some of the ideas I'd had early on were rapidly ditched – such as some weird demons for one of the early storylines.'

A decision was made early on in the production meetings that the special-effects budget would be much more effectively spent on digital manipulation than on computer animation. Computer animation is the most time-intensive and expensive weapon in the effects arsenal. Effects like these are costly because they involve the creation of 3-D models, the application of textures and real-world lighting, and eventual frame-by-frame animation. Think dinosaurs in *Jurassic Park,* Jar Jar Binks in *Star Wars: The Phantom Menace* or various alien creatures in *Evolution.* Digital manipulation, however, uses specially shot 'real-world' footage which is then blended with other images, enhanced, and manipulated in order to create the desired effect. It is much less time-consuming (and hence much less expensive) than computer animation, and usually ends up looking more authentic.

The first series of *Randall & Hopkirk (Deceased)* had something like 650 digital effects shots spread across six episodes – that's over a hundred per episode. Series two has about the same level. They range, of course, from the more obvious – Marty's materializations, the wholesale destruction of small English villages – to the subtle and almost unnoticeable.

Simon Wright is effusive in his praise of Double Negative. 'I can't tell you how skilled they are. They are pretty much the best in the world. We've got our own rooms in Double Negative working full-time on the series. They've set the style and the design of it. I don't think – ever – have we had such high-quality film effects just made for television. We are very, very lucky.'

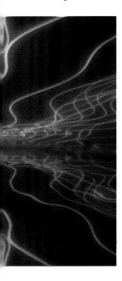

Opposite: A collection of images showing Double Negative's skills in digital manipulation, including Sidney Crabbe's intrusion into Wyvern's room ('A Blast From The Past'), Harry Wallis's descent into Hell from the same episode, the computer game Marty plays in 'Drop Dead', the added background film to a driving sequence and the Pawns from 'Marshall & Snellgrove'.

Special effects – Marty's materializations

In a series about a ghost there has to be a way for the audience to be able to tell that he or she is a ghost – otherwise what's the point? But how to do it without the whole thing looking silly or cheap, that's the question.

In the original version of *Randall & Hopkirk (Deceased)* – made in the days before computer-generated special effects – Marty's appearances and disappearances were limited to what television people call freeze-frame 'lock-offs' – an old-school visual effect that's been in use since the days of the Keystone Cops. The cast would freeze mid-sentence, the camera would be locked in place so it didn't shift or wobble (unlike the actors, most of the time), and Kenneth Cope would walk off set so the camera could be started up again. The finished effect was a scene where Marty would instantaneously appear or disappear, usually accompanied by a pinging sound effect.

Thirty years later and, ironically, it's the same technique that's used to get Marty in and out of shot. However, using the power of computers, Marty's entrances and exits can be disguised. All manner of clever effects could be used, from a straight fade in and fade out to an all-out multi-media extravaganza involving tartan fireworks and showers of flowers. So, which one to choose?

The first question was the most basic: whether or not Marty Hopkirk would be semi-transparent throughout the series.

'We gave this a lot of thought,' says Double Negative's Matthew Holben, 'but in the end we decided to have Marty transparent only when he materialized and dematerialized. What makes these characters come alive is the way Vic and Bob spark off each other, and we didn't want to lose the immediacy of their performances. If we went down the route of having Vic see-through for the entire series, Vic and Bob would never have been filmed together because all of Vic's shots would have had to be done against a blue backdrop. Not only that, but by this stage we were already getting jittery

about how much time we had to complete the shooting. There simply wasn't the time or resource to do all of Vic's scenes in post-production.'

So with the decision made to keep Marty's ghost transparent only at the beginning and end of his scenes, how did the effects artists create his materialization? In fact, the Double Negative team wanted to create a generic effect that could be used throughout the entire series, yet would be interesting and varied enough to capture the imagination of the viewers each time Marty appeared.

'We wanted to do something that hadn't been done before,' Matthew Holben remembers. 'Charlie had an enormous amount of input in helping us conceptualize these sequences, and it was by working together with him, Mark [Mylod] and Rachel [Talalay] that we decided on the particle animation and shimmering effect that make up Marty's materialization.'

The final effect has Marty wafting on as a cloud of ectoplasmic material which gradually coalesces into his white-clad form, but such things as the shape of the cloud, the speed of coalescence and which bits of Marty we see first can all be altered. The beauty of Double Negative's approach means that, once the original animation had been created, it can, with minor tweaking to its 'parameters' – be used over and over without any sense of repetition.

Which is more than can be said for Kenneth Cope's materializations in the original series.

Left: Marty dematerializes in the Radlands School chapel ('The Best Years of Your Death').

Below: Marty surprises his old friend Jeff by appearing at his own graveside in 'Drop Dead'.

IN
LOVING MEMORY
- OF -
MARTY HOPKIRK
FAITHFUL
UNTO DEATH

Special effects – Wyvern's room

'I created all this so you would feel at home,' says Wyvern, reclining in his armchair in an ornate and fusty library during his first encounter with Marty. But this is no ordinary room. As a figment of their joint imaginations, the room shifts in and out of reality, the walls gently undulating and waving like tall grasses in a breeze.

The vision for the room first came from Production Designer Grenville Horner.

'I'd been looking through some old David Hockney prints,' says Grenville, 'and was struck by the strange otherworldliness of his photomontages. Overall, these pictures create an image, but since they're made up of all these smaller, slightly disjointed pictures you get a strange dislocated sense of reality. Because Wyvern's room is a pastiche of what a library should look like, we wondered how we could apply Hockney's technique to a three-dimensional space.'

With this vision in mind, Grenville set about finding a real room that would do as the basis for the Wyvern's study. After much scouting around, he discovered the library in the Sir John Soane's Museum in London.

'We wanted to find somewhere that was

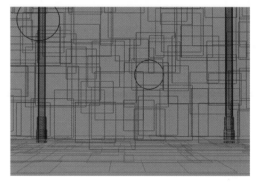

The various elements that comprise Wyvern's mysterious room – only the actors and the furniture are real: the rest has been constructed within the memory of a computer.

immensely intricate,' recalled Grenville. 'This library was perfect. Architecturally, it was a beautiful shape with these high, vaulted arches and inset coves. It was also filled with the most amazing stuff – clocks, book, pictures, statues. Everyone agreed it was the ideal location, so we set about taking a few pictures so we could build up the montage.'

A 'few pictures' eventually ran to over 300 stills of the room. Once all the pictures were digitized into Double Negative's computer system, the modelling started. Each individual picture – representing one feature of the room – was converted into a 'particle', and all of the particles were then assembled, like an electronic Lego set,

into the shape of a room. Unlike real Lego, however, these particles can shift and move according to a set of pre-defined rules.

'Whereas Hockney's montages are static, ours were dynamic,' notes Double Negative's Matthew Holben. 'We were able to apply rules of elasticity and attractiveness to each particle so they would behave intelligently with other elements in the room.' A good example of these behaviours are when Marty and Wyvern are bashing a cricket ball around the study. In one shot, Wyvern hits the ball alongside a wall, and as the ball whizzes past the camera, the wall particles are blown away in its path, in much the same way as a pile of leaves gets disturbed when a car drives though it. But unlike the leaves, the wall particles slowly spring back into shape, as if held together by pieces of elastic.

Once the behaviour of the room had been established, it was time to get Vic Reeves and Tom Baker inside it. All of their scenes were shot on a blue background, and for the scenes in Wyvern's room, the crew used tracking markers on the camera. This meant that if, during a scene, the camera started at position A, high above the two actors, and then swept down and around them to a lower point B, the same 'virtual movement' could be replicated in the electronic world of Wyvern's room. Once the two images were blended together – the real-world footage and the electronic study – the illusion was complete. A strange, dislocated virtual world where the walls of the room are gossamer thin and seem to float in a light breeze.

'It was a real thrill seeing it all work,' remembers Grenville Horner. 'We deconstructed this quintessentially English library and then reconstructed it again as a piece of fantasy. It was extraordinary to see this Hockney-esque idiom move into three dimensions.'

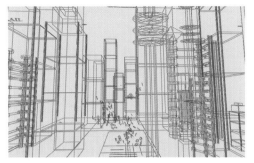
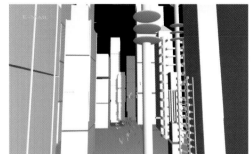

Data City

In the episode 'O Happy Isle', Marty is called upon to pull data out of a computer. He'd done the same kind of thing previously, in 'A Blast from the Past', but there was a feeling that the effects used then could be improved upon.

'The script read as if Marty was going through a pipe with data whizzing past, but that can look pretty tacky,' says Matthew Holben. 'What we wanted to represent was the electronic interior of a CPU, with Marty systematically passing through it and looking for information. We wanted to get a sense of movement through a structure, so we came up with towers of scrolling information to give it depth and interest.'

The 'towers of information' were created within Double Negative's computers, which shows how technology has improved. Faced with a similar problem in the past, Matthew had been forced to adopt a less elegant solution.

'We did a film called *Hackers* many years ago where, to put across the idea of being inside a computer's memory, we had to actually build transparent towers of perspex and project images of data on to them!'

The various elements that go to make up Data City – the cyberspacial conglomeration of information that Marty navigates through in 'O Happy Isle'.

The Burning Man

Harriet Banks-Smith's final moments in 'The Best Years of Your Death' were realized by setting a stuntman on fire. The burning ghost that turns up in 'Whatever Possessed You', and again as a dream image in 'Revenge of the Bog People' was achieved in a slightly more technological way.

'One of the things we decided very early on,' Matthew Holben explains, 'was that it had to be a very ethereal, unreal image. It couldn't be real burning flesh, because you're then getting into something that can't be shown on the BBC.'

Having taken the constraints of time, budget and good taste into account, Matthew made his recommendations to Charlie Higson and Metin Huseyin over how the effect could be achieved. 'We figured out we needed an animation guide, so we put a mime artist in an orange suit – orange because we knew that was the colour of the flames we were going to go for, and we could get a lot of bounce light off him and reflected around the set.'

The mime artist was just there as a guide: the poor man was completely removed in post-production and replaced with a three-dimensional, human-shaped, computer-generated mannequin.

'We did a lot of research and development,' explains Matthew, 'on how we could cover the mannequin with computer-generated flames. If you hold a candle up and move it through the air the flame alters its shape, and we had to take all that into account.'

The final image – a burning figure wrestling with Marty across a hotel room – is one of the trickiest, and most impressive, effects shots that Double Negative have been asked to do in the series.

Opposite and below: To create the fiery-ghost effect for Roger Whale's meeting with the Burning Man in 'Whatever Possessed You', a mime artist in an orange bodysuit first performed all the moves. Double Negative then replaced this visual reference with a 3-D model.

Incidental music

Music can make or break a screen production. Eric Clapton's plangent guitar is the thing that most people remember about cult BBC serial *Edge of Darkness*, while *Star Wars* might have been just another *Ice Pirates* without John Williams's rousing score. Choosing a distinctive sound for *Randall & Hopkirk (Deceased)* could have proven critical to the success or failure of the series.

With most series, the title music and the incidental music are both written by the same composer, but a decision was taken early on to split the soundtrack into three. David Arnold would compose the main theme, while Murray Gold's incidental music would be punctuated by contemporary songs from well-known British bands, specially commissioned for the series.

'The songs were courtesy of Nick Angel,' Charlie Higson says, 'who now works full-time for Working Title Films organizing music for soundtracks. I'd always wanted to have a lush orchestral score, and I knew we didn't have the budget for that. What I needed was to get an injection of some extra funds from another source, so we set about setting up a soundtrack album.'

The songs (later collected together on the soundtrack album) were contributed by Britpop stars such as Basement Jaxx, The Orb and The Charlatans. They came and went in the series, adding atmosphere without being memorable, but it was the haunting, Sixties-influenced track 'My Body May Die', performed by Pulp and, bizarrely, The Swingle Sisters, that would set the tone for the entire show.

'Pulp had said they would write a song especially for us,' Charlie recalls. 'We wanted to set up a song in the first episode that was associated with Marty – it was his theme song. That was Bob's idea.'

With David Arnold's theme and Pulp's iconic song in place, only the incidental music was left.

'We had those two pieces of music,' Charlie continues, 'and then we needed a composer to do the rest. We wanted the music to be distinctive, so that when you heard it you always knew what it was you were watching.'

The chosen composer was Murray Gold – already well known for his soundtrack to the BBC TV adaptation of *Vanity Fair.*

'Murray was very excited about the idea of doing it orchestrally, and he was very keen on having themes for characters and situations that would recur and could be reworked all the way through the series. As well as his own original material, which had a fantastic kind of magical resonance to it, he wrote various stings and pieces based on the David Arnold theme, and he wrote various themes based on the Pulp song.'

As always in film and television, nobody ever has enough time to do as much as they would like. Music is usually the loser in this process, given that it's almost the last thing to be commissioned.

'As everything was done quite late and in a bit of a hurry, by episode three Murray gave us a kit of bits and pieces, and said, "Here, make up your music out of that",' Charlie recalls. 'So I ended up working with Colin Chapman, the sound editor, creating a soundtrack where none had existed. Series two he's had longer on, and while we're going with the same style he'll be doing more of it synthetically.'

Sadly, the soundtrack album doesn't contain any of Murray Gold's music. What it does contain is a vocal arrangement of David Arnold's theme tune sung by Nina Persson (lead vocalist from The Cardigans) – a version heard in the episode 'Revenge of the Bog People'. This song could, however, have been different. Dramatically different.

'Originally,' Charlie reveals, 'we wanted to get Vic to do a duet with someone. Bob suggested we do something based on the David Arnold music, as it was such a good piece.' He shakes his head at the ludicrousness of the idea. 'We tried working it as a duet, but it wasn't the kind of style that suited Vic.'

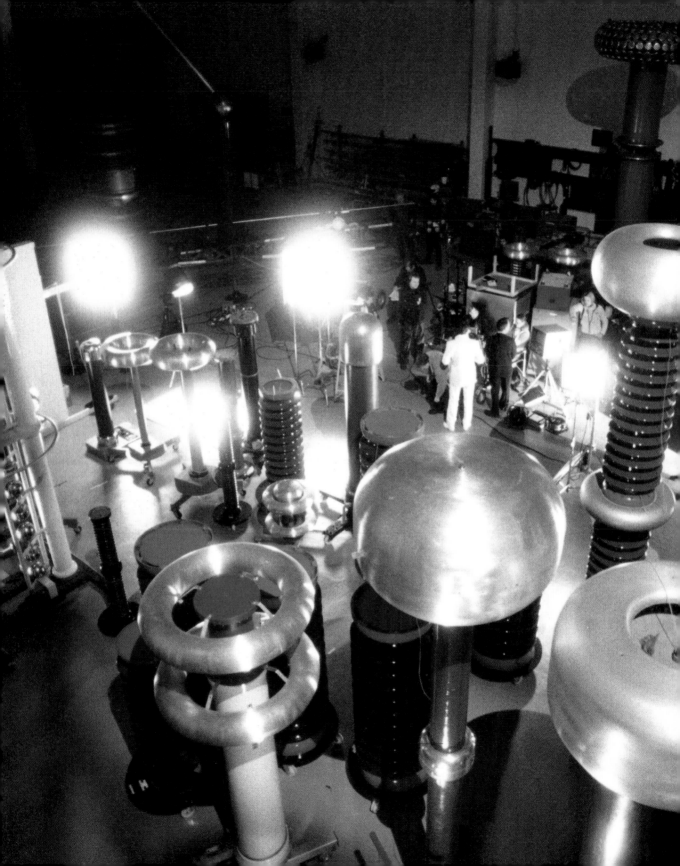

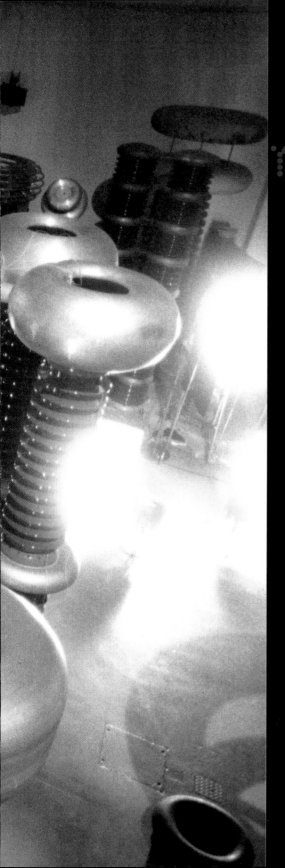

randall & hopkirk (deceased)

the episodes

Thirteen episodes. Six writers. Four directors. Just under eleven hours of television. That's what all the activity – the thousands of hours of work undertaken by hundreds of people – have ultimately come down to.

And it's all that the audience ever sees. It's what they judge the series on. Regardless of the countless minor dramas that have gone on behind the scenes, it's only the final images that reach our TV screens that make up what we know as *Randall & Hopkirk (Deceased)*.

drop dead

Written by Charlie Higson. Directed by Mark Mylod

Art. What is it? A painting, a sculpture, perhaps even a performance can be art, but what about death? Can murder be art? And if it can, doesn't that make the detective just a jumped-up art critic?

Jeff and Marty (more properly, Randall & Hopkirk Security Services) are employed on yet another divorce case – this time involving a man named Kenneth Crisby. It all goes terribly wrong, and the trio (Jeannie, Marty's fiancée, is there as well) have to make a rapid escape, pursued by an imprecation-hurling Crisby.

Back in their offices, depressed at the way fate keeps on handing them divorce cases, the detective duo find themselves hired by cutting-edge artist Gordon Stylus. He's afraid his wife Annette might commit suicide, and he wants them to watch over her.

Jeff and Marty are invited to a party Stylus is throwing for Annette in his mansion by the coast – the day before Marty's marriage – but at the party it becomes all too clear that Stylus is self-obsessed to the point where he can't see how depressed Annette is. Talking to one of the guests while Stylus creates an artwork 'live' while dressed as a robot, Jeff discovers that Annette is rumoured to be the creative force behind Gordon's success, the one who stays home painting while he swans around parties.

Marty, meanwhile, has been talking to Annette, but through a bizarre set of coincidences he ends up on the bonnet of her car. He has little time to appreciate his precarious position before she apparently drives off the edge of a cliff, killing them both.

At the church, the next day, Jeannie is told by Inspector Large and Sergeant Liddel that Marty's body has been discovered.

Marty is buried. Jeff and Jeannie mourn. And then Marty comes back as a ghost for one night only, in order to solve his own death; shocking Jeff, who is still trying to come to terms with his partner's death when Marty appears in front of

> 'Marty, if we were going any slower we'd be parking!'
>
> Jeff

him again in a graveyard.

Marty remembers someone getting out of the car just before it plunged over the cliff. Jeff has discovered that the infidelious Kenneth Crisby is Stylus's agent. It's all beginning to come together…

Jeff and Marty go to confront Stylus, but Crisby is there. He knocks Jeff out and together he and Stylus tie Jeff to a wire frame above a vat of resin. Jeff's about to be turned into a life-size work of art.

The true details of the plot all come out. Annette was about to go public with the truth that she made most of Stylus's paintings. Neither Stylus nor Crisby could afford for that to happen. And Crisby wanted revenge on two meddling detectives: what a perfect opportunity to kill two birds with one stone. All it took was for Stylus to set up a perfect alibi, with a robot creating a work of art in his place, and for him then to knock Annette out and put her in her own car before driving it away and letting it roll over the edge of a cliff…

Marty knocks out Crisby with his psychic powers, but it is nearing daybreak and he has to return to his grave. Jeannie, who has followed Jeff, is menaced by a chainsaw-wielding robot controlled by Stylus, but Marty returns dramatically and turns the robot on Stylus.

Marty's actions in returning mean that the grave has rejected him. The afterlife is not for him. He and Jeff are still a team!

First episodes are always slightly schizophrenic: they have to set up characters and situations and give the audience an idea of what the series is likely to be about whilst still attempting to convey a plot. It's not surprising, therefore, that, despite its amazing production values and popularity with fans, Charlie Higson has mixed feelings about 'Drop Dead' (originally entitled 'The Simple Art of Murder').

'It was the first one I wrote,' Charlie says, 'because we had to do a pilot episode – we were going to do a one-off and then if it went well do a series, but because of people's time availability it

Above: Kenneth Crisby (Charles Dance) poses with a crowbar in front of a self-portrait of his client, Gordon Stylus, moments before attempting to commit an act of artistic vandalism on Jeff.
Opposite top: Jeff and Jeannie enjoying themselves at Annette Stylus's party, unaware of the tragedy about to overtake them.
Opposite bottom: Gordon and Annette Stylus (David Tennant and Hanna Miles).

wasn't an option. Looking back, I probably tried to put too much into it. Maybe, down the line, once we'd written all the other ones I should have just thrown it out and done a completely new first episode.'

In fact, Charlie ended up writing and rewriting the episode, constantly honing it in an effort to get everything in. 'It changed drastically,' he says. 'It went through hundreds of drafts and changes. The original scripts were more spectacular on the action front than we ended up doing. There were more instances of Marty nearly dying – there were bits of him climbing around on the outside of the building and things falling off. It still is a bit complicated for a first episode in terms of the motivations of the various villains. But it probably repays more than one viewing.'

Other things begin to emerge when the episode is watched a number of times. Some of the works of art in Stylus's studio are pastiches of well-known contemporary artists, for instance – Gilbert and George (the stained-glass-effect wedding portrait), Marc Quinn (the sculpture of Stylus's head done in frozen urine, except that Quinn used blood), Damien Hirst (Stylus himself, cut in half, except that Hirst uses sharks and cows). Many of the works were created by one man – Brian Williams.

'He's a very talented artist,' says Production Designer Grenville Horner, 'and when we asked him if he wanted to get involved he jumped at the chance. Most of the stuff you see in the show is his, and we even commissioned him to do portraits of Stylus and Annette for the chainsaw scene.'

The episode makes fun of modern art, rather than celebrating it, and it's a courageous artist who would allow his work to be pilloried on national television. Let alone ripped apart by a chainsaw. But, as Grenville Horner points out, Williams saw the advantages…

'Brian was overjoyed to be able to get all his work hanging for the exhibition scene – it was like his own private installation, and it really did look

Opposite: *Marty undertakes some close-range detection – who exactly is driving the car that's just about to plunge over the cliff, taking him with it?*
Below left: *A couple of art critics suspect that Gordon Stylus's work is not his own. The man on the right should know – he's Brian Williams who painted all the art for this episode.*

HITCHED in EDEN

quite stunning. The space was enormous – the biggest space I've ever seen – and not something that every artist gets access to. It was like stepping into Andy Warhol's Factory. Believe it or not, Brian even managed to sell some of his work during the shoot. Charlie bought a couple of his pictures, I think.'

It's almost *de rigueur* in a revival, remake or re-imagining of an old series to make some kind of passing reference to the original version, and *Randall & Hopkirk (Deceased)* was no exception.

'We put in a lot of little nods to the original series in that first episode,' Charlie admits. 'We were trying to have a bit of fun, and to let the fans of the original series know that we had a certain respect for it and we weren't trying to completely desecrate it. The poem that Marty quotes is the same as in the original, of course, and there's a bit at the beginning where Jeff's got a map and we think he's plotting some kind of elaborate detective work, but actually he's plotting Marty's wedding, and all the street names relate to people who were involved with the original series. We also got Vic to adopt the same startled pose that's

drop dead 121

used by Kenneth Cope in the first episode and in the credits of the original series, and of course it's a double bluff because the car doesn't actually kill him at that point. Their offices are in Cope House, of course, and one of the villains is called Kenneth.'

The critical first episode of the series was directed by Mark Mylod, who had been chosen following an extensive search for a director with the right set of qualities. 'We saw a lot of directors for the first series,' says Charlie, 'from very experienced TV drama directors to commercials directors who'd never done any television at all. We decided we needed someone in the middle, someone who had solid TV experience but also had larger ambitions and was interested in trying new stuff. Plus they also had to have a strong flair for comedy, and to be able to work with Vic and Bob. The obvious candidate was Mark. He had directed *Shooting Stars* and *Bang Bang It's Reeves and Mortimer*, Vic and Bob were comfortable working with him, I'd worked with him on *The Fast Show*, and he'd also done *Cold Feet*, so we knew he was OK handling larger scale drama. And he'd done good work with *The Royle Family*.'

Compared with later episodes, 'Drop Dead' is remarkably free of well-known faces. Mark Gatiss and Steve Pemberton (from BBC's *The League of Gentlemen*), make a cameo appearance as policemen, and Jessica Stevenson (better known for her work co-writing and co-starring in Channel 4's sitcom *Spaced*) appears as Marty and Jeff's receptionist Felia.

'What I wanted was to set up a receptionist in the first episode who then leaves, so Jeannie temporarily comes in to fill the post, and then she slowly becomes part of the company,' Charlie remembers. 'In the original script of episode one, their receptionist had been some terrible old battleaxe who scared off all their clients, and who neither Jeff nor Marty had the courage to sack. Bob didn't like this character so we changed it to a receptionist who was pregnant and was leaving to have the baby. We saw quite a few people for

it, but when Jessica came in she was the only one who played Felia as Eastern European. And she played her in a very glum, dead-pan way which was very funny. And I thought, "I wish I'd written a lot more for this character," but we were set by then.'

Dwarfing Gatiss, Pemberton and Stevenson is the charismatic figure of Charles Dance, making a rare television appearance in the plum role of Kenneth Crisby.

Above: *Jeannie and her sister Wendy (Melissa Knatchbull) at Marty's funeral.*
Opposite top: *Charles Dance as Kenneth Crisby.*
Opposite bottom: *Jeff Randall confronts Stylus in his studio.*

'He really is a fantastic actor,' Simon Wright enthuses. 'He walked through that part. What was really interesting was to have two former comedians, or people hitherto only known as comedians, suddenly standing there on screen with Britain's greatest actor of his generation.'

'I don't usually get asked to do stuff like this,' Charles Dance reveals, 'which is a shame, because I love it. The last thing I did that had laughs in it was a play about twelve years ago, so when Charlie asked me if I wanted to get involved I jumped at the opportunity. It was too good to pass up. It all started when I was doing a play with Millie Fox in 1998. Charlie and Simon came down to see Millie and we got chatting about the series. The deal was they'd have a guest baddie each weekend and when we got talking about the series and the parts in it, it was as if the Crisby role had been written for me. I loved it. There's a wonderful over-the-top cartoon quality to the character that I instantly liked, and working with Vic and Bob was a great opportunity to have some fun with some very talented people.'

It wasn't all fun, however. In the fight sequence near the end, Crisby gets a can of paint flung in his face. Unfortunately, there was a mix up in the props department, and instead of being covered with a special water-soluble stage paint, Dance got a face full of Dulux Satin Sheen Emulsion.

'It was desperately embarrassing,' said Grenville Horner. 'Charles was very good about it and didn't make a fuss at all but it took him hours to get the paint off and it looked horribly uncomfortable. That's one incident I think I'll leave off my résumé.'

> *Afore the sun shall rise anew,*
> *Each ghost into his grave must... geuw,*
> *Cursed be the ghost who dares to stay,*
> *And face the awful light of day.*
> *Ye shall not your grave return,*
> *Until your chosen one is... geurn.*

mental apparition disorder

Written by Charlie Higson, based on
an original story by Mike Pratt and
Ian Wilson. Directed by Rachel Talalay

*Obsession is a terrible thing. A man can be so
obsessed with gambling that he steals in order
to fund his habit. A woman can be so obsessed
with another man that she resorts to petty theft
to attract his attention. And a man might be so
obsessed with the memory of his dead friend that
he starts seeing his ghost wherever he goes…*

Somewhere in Limbo it has been decided that
Marty Hopkirk will need some help if he is to
move on to the next plane of existence, and so he
is assigned to the care of Mr Wyvern – a genial
soul whose speciality is in assisting spirits to
expand their powers and come to terms with their
fate. Pretty soon, however, Wyvern realizes that
Marty is going to be a challenging case…

Jeff is hired by the head of security at a nearby
casino – a man with the unlikely nickname of
Three-Piece – to investigate thefts from the till.
Three-Piece thinks that a waitress named Karen is
responsible, but he has feelings for her that he is
too nervous to express, and he doesn't want to
confront her. In fact, he's been covering for her,
but things are beginning to get out of hand and he
needs the problem solved.

Jeff wants to help Three-Piece, but he's too tied
up in getting the office receptionist, Felia, to
hospital – she's unexpectedly gone into labour,
and there are some concerns that the child might
be a mutant. Jeff has recently asked Jeannie to
help out at the agency, so she agrees to handle the
case.

The stress of continually seeing Marty is
beginning to tell on Jeff. He confides in Jeannie,
and she asks her sister Wendy for help. Together,
they arrange for Jeff to be sent off to Trilby Park –
a sanatorium run by the urbane Doctor Lawyer.

Doctor Lawyer's method is to use hypnotism
and relaxation techniques to send his patients into
a trance, during which he can treat whatever
obsessive/compulsive disorders they might be
suffering from. What none of them are aware of,
however, is that while they are unconscious he
tortures them and implants post-hypnotic
suggestions that they steal for him.

Jeannie goes undercover at the casino to watch
Karen, and not only discovers that Karen is indeed

a thief, but also that she is stealing the money in order to make Three-Piece pay attention to her – she has feelings for him as well, but is too shy to tell him. Jeannie gets them together, but is surprised to see Doctor Lawyer gambling at the casino. He's racking up huge debts, and is having problems paying them…

Doctor Lawyer's treatment is having its effect on Jeff – he is refusing to acknowledge Marty's existence. Marty, in turn, is fading away. According to Wyvern, Marty will soon become a mindless gibbering spirit if the situation is not reversed.

Lawyer discovers that Jeff is a detective, and is considering killing him when Jeannie turns up. During a confrontation, Lawyer uses the sanatorium's public-address system to order the hypnotized patients to attack Jeff and Jeannie, but a fading Marty manages to imitate Lawyer's voice and orders the residents to attack the doctor instead.

With Lawyer disabled, if not dead, Jeff decides to accept Marty for what he is – a supremely bothersome ghost.

'Mental Apparition Disorder' (originally called 'You Don't Have to be Mad to Work Here') is the only one of the new *Randall & Hopkirk (Deceased)* episodes to be based on an idea from the original 1970s series. As Simon Wright explains, there were some plots that just couldn't be avoided.

'The first episode is clearly similar,' he says, 'because Marty has to be alive at the beginning, he has to die, and then he has to solve the mystery of his own death, as it were. But the next, and only, logical step is Jeff coming to terms with the fact that he does have this ghost around, which we chose to do straight away, because the sooner you settle all those questions, and Jeff – and all of us – have acceptance of Marty and the world they're inhabiting, the better.'

Above: *Lucy English (Fiona Allen) fixes trancelike on a pair of antique daggers belonging to Craig Nash (a cameo appearance by Martin Clunes) just prior to plunging them into his heart.*
Opposite bottom: *Felia (Jessica Stevenson) goes into labour.*

'I didn't watch the original episode or read the script,' Charlie Higson confesses, 'but I took the basic storyline because I thought it was interesting.'

The episode was directed by Rachel Talalay – an experienced Hollywood film director (*Tank Girl, Freddie's Dead: The Final Nightmare*) who had also worked in American television on *Ally McBeal* and in British television on *Band of Gold* and *Touching Evil*.

'There were several reasons for asking Rachel to direct,' Simon Wright explains. 'One was the fact that she was American – she has a slightly different sensibility. She, like all American directors, loves pace and knows how to direct action. She also has huge experience in special effects: she conceived and produced *The Borrowers* as a movie. So she really did understand what was possible and what wasn't possible. We had no experience in that field whatsoever, and she had fantastic experience. We were still to some extent exploring where we were going with the whole thing. When she saw *Randall & Hopkirk (Deceased)* she realized that this was something nobody had ever done before, or certainly not in the last twenty years: that sort of high-concept television, which we were used to in the 1970s with *The A Team* and *The Dukes of Hazzard*, has disappeared out of the world market. And to come back and do a television series so ambitious, and so different, and so exciting, was something she saw as really challenging. She would have done more of the second series had she been available and we would have loved to have had her back.'

This episode, more than most of the others, showcases a number of well-known British actors. Richard Todd (of *Dambusters* fame) and Wanda Ventham (veteran of many ITC series, as well as Gerry Anderson's *UFO*), both play patients at the clinic, while comedy actors Hugh Laurie (whose credits range from Hollywood films such as *101 Dalmatians* and *Stuart Little* to British television series such as *Jeeves and Wooster*) and Martin

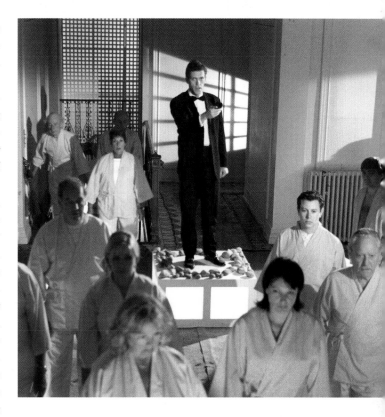

Clunes (*Men Behaving Badly*) play Doctor Lawyer and a victim of his schemes respectively. Well-known actress Fiona Allen appears as a nymphomaniac victim of Doctor Lawyer's scheme, but perhaps the oddest casting is that of writer/director/actor Stephen Berkoff as the apparently disembodied mouth that owns the casino. Berkoff's credits range from action films along the lines of *Beverly Hills Cop* and *Octopussy* to fringe theatrical events that include his own adaptation of Franz Kafka's *Metamorphosis*. Let it not be forgotten, however, that he also appeared in Gerry Anderson's *UFO* as an Interceptor pilot...

Doctor Lawyer (Hugh Laurie) directs his patients to attack Je: and Jeannie.

> *Well met, good traveller, be at peace,*
> *Sit down with me and tell thy tale,*
> *acome join me for a noble feast,*
> *Good cheer to thee I can avail,*
> *My welcome hearthside is thy lease,*
> *Enter my home and rest a... whale.*

'I'm sorry about this,
Mr Randall, but I've been
under a lot of pressure
and I think I may
have gone mad.'
Doctor Lawyer

the best years of
your death

Written by Charlie Higson. Directed by Mark Mylod

A green, unpleasant land. White-clad figures on a green cricket pitch. Midnight feasts in the dorm. Latin lessons and prep. Wars are won and lost on the playing fields of our public schools – sometimes literally.

A teacher is beheaded by cowled figures during a bizarre late-night service in the chapel of Radlands public school. His head plops into a jar of preserving fluid, alongside that of the school's matron. Death, it would appear, is on the curriculum…

Jeannie visits her sister and brother-in-law in their country house. They seem as settled and as superior as ever, but Jeannie soon starts to worry about her nephew Daniel, who's home from school for the weekend. He used to be as rambunctious as any teenager, but now he's buttoned down and as rigid as a soldier on parade. Blazer neat, homework complete, manner polite, but underneath it all she senses a desperate loneliness.

She's right to suspect something: before Jeannie leaves, Daniel passes her a note telling her that 'they' killed a teacher at his school, although he never gets a chance to tell her who 'they' are.

At the office, Jeannie shares the note with Jeff and confides her concerns. Jeff, eager to help, suggests they investigate.

They apply for the newly vacant posts of teacher and matron and, with Marty's help, they get them. The only catch is – they have to pretend to be married!

The two of them are soon ensconced at Radlands, and realize pretty quickly that there is something odd going on. Headmaster Captain Graves is a martinet; the man-hating Head Matron, Harriet Banks-Smith, runs the school with a rod of iron, and the boys act older and more worldly than their age.

Events come to a head when the Radlands boys search Jeff and Jeannie's room and discover they are not who they say they are. Jeannie is taken prisoner by them, and held in the chapel. Jeff, under Marty's control, tries to rescue her, but is also taken captive. The boys are under the influence of the Head Matron, who is having an affair with Captain Graves. When anyone discovers the truth about the affair... they are disposed of by the boys.

Under the horrified gaze of Graves, who knew nothing of the bizarre cult of worship that the matron had built around herself, Banks-Smith stirs the boys up against Jeff and Jeannie. Daniel, acting as the voice of reason, pulls the boys back from the brink of madness, and Marty terrifies Banks-Smith by taking over the head of the dead teacher and talking to her. She stumbles into an oil lamp, catches fire, and burns to death.

The original series of *Randall & Hopkirk (Deceased)* seemed to take a grim delight in

'Strict discipline makes it easier to...eat boys' heads!'

Prospective teacher

Above: *Captain Graves (Peter Bowles) presents one face in public, but another one entirely in private. No prizes for guessing who Head Matron, Harriet Banks-Smith (Phyllis Logan), is secretly in love with...*
Opposite: *Harriet Banks-Smith reflects on the sins of small boys.*
Left: *Prospective teachers, awaiting their interviews with Captain Graves. (Right: Andrew McGibbon. Centre: Anthony Daniels, better known as Star Wars' C-3PO.)*

Right: Jeff finds himself in the frustrating position of being in bed with Jeannie and unable to take advantage of the situation. Jeannie has yet to discover that he snores. Her reading matter is written by… Charlie Higson.
Below right: Mike Nicholson's storyboards show Marty taking possession of a pigeon.
Opposite top: The pupils of Radlands School have fallen under the spell of their Matron – a harridan who believes that all boys are dirty and need to be punished.
Opposite middle: Jeannie's nephew, Danny (Rory Jennings).
Opposite bottom: Marty takes over Jeff's body in an ultimately unproductive attempt to seduce Jeannie.

downbeat locations: dingy hotel corridors, seedy offices, abandoned factories and so on (most of which were located in the Elstree back lot). The new series takes the opposite approach: setting each story in a self-contained, isolated location, suggestive of idealized Britishness, from which the characters rarely depart. 'The Best Years of Your Death' is a prime example. Here the location is Radlands School: the kind of place that has a niche in the British psyche and yet hardly even exists any more, except as an anachronistic reminder of the past. Crimson blazers, school chapel, cricketing flannels… it's all too good to be true.

And there's a worm in this Eden. Again, whereas the original series had petty criminals and minor villains as its antagonists, here the trouble is caused from the inside. Suppressed teenage sexuality and subservience to authority are the villains here.

A fine cast of British stalwarts was assembled to bring the various characters in 'The Best Days of Your Death' to… er… life. Peter Bowles – a fine actor who appeared as a stock villain in many ITC series of the late 1960s and early 1970s (*The Avengers*, *Danger Man*, *The Persuaders*) before finding fame in comedy series such as *To the*

Manor Born – plays the school's headmaster, Captain Graves, with nostril-flaring, evangelical fire. Supporting him is Phyllis Logan, a Scottish actress equally at home playing Lady Jane Felsham in *Lovejoy* and an RAF pilot in pulp science-fiction serial *Invasion: Earth*. Watch out also for Anthony Daniels, putting in a rare performance out of C-3PO's golden armour, as Mr Walton – one of the unlucky applicants for the teaching post that Jeff, with Marty's ghostly assistance, manages to secure.

One member of the cast in particular had worked with Charlie Higson before. 'The central kid we used as Wendy's son, Danny, was Rory Jennings who we used on *The Fast Show* for the Competitive Dad sketches,' says Charlie, 'since he was very small, and he's always been the most fantastically natural actor. He's not a stage-school kid at all.'

As with many of Charlie Higson's scripts, there's a running theme to the character names in this episode. Many of them are references to TV critics – with Nancy Banks-Smith, A.A. Gill, Charlie Catchpole and Gary Bushell all having their surnames appropriated. 'If you make up a

name it always sounds made up,' Charlie says, 'but if you've got a schematic it gives you something to hang the names on.'

Despite the obvious strengths in the performances and the direction, Charlie does have some regrets about the episode.

'We ran out of time,' he concedes. 'There were a lot of things that were tied up more in the script. It's one of the episodes where it's best not to think too much about what happens afterwards. The school incident would be all over the press for months, and Jeff and Jeannie would be at the centre of it all as the people who went in and solved it, but they're still carrying on in anonymity.'

Perhaps it was the lack of time that explains the rather 'adult' nature of the opening sequence – a scene that wouldn't have been out of place in a George Romero zombie movie...

'The episode opens with the teacher's head being decapitated,' laughs Simon Wright. 'The BBC had complaints, and as a result the Editorial Management Board had to meet. When we repeat the episode we're going to have to cut that shot.'

> *If a beast you want to be,*
> *The secret of its heart unfurl.*
> *A stronger mind is all you'll need,*
> *To possess its very... seurl.*

paranoia

Written by Charlie Higson and Paul Whitehouse.
Directed by Charlie Higson

Some people believe that history is a web of hidden connections between seemingly isolated events. Others believe that it's a morass of mistakes and blunders held together by blind luck. Under normal circumstances, these two sets of people never get together. Under normal circumstances…

Douglas Milton, a former civil servant and current whistle-blower on Government corruption, is scheduled to give a speech at a conference on conspiracies. He's nervous that he might be the target of assassins – especially since he has the only manuscript of his potentially blockbusting exposé of crime and secret double-dealing in his possession. So he hires Jeff and Jeannie to protect him.

He's right to do so. The list of people who want him dead is pretty long. There's the Hammers of God – a crypto-Fascist organization who want to strike a blow against the system. There's the British Government itself, in the shape of civil servants Lacey and Bulstrode, who hire an incompetent assassin named Swift to kill him. There's his loving wife, who hires svelte assassin Magda to kill her husband on the basis that the manuscript would be worth more if its author had been mysteriously killed. There's his former mistress, Annabel, whose reason has become totally unhinged by his rejection of her and who goes round talking to a teddy bear while holding a sharp pair of scissors. Finally, there's the team of fanatics from an unspecified Middle Eastern country who are on their way to the hotel with what might be a bomb in their possession.

Jeff and Jeannie arrive at the hotel with Milton, and pretty quickly get involved with various unlikely companions. Jeannie finds herself – not unwillingly – being chatted up by the conference's head of security, Richard Shelley, while Jeff himself is pursued by Magda; realizing that Jeff has the book for safe-keeping, she manoeuvres Jeff into his bedroom so she can search for it.

During the run-up to Milton's speech, most of the guest cast are killed off in various ways. One member of the Hammers of God is killed when the hotel's new electric fence sets off the dynamite he is holding. Another Hammers of God member is accidentally shot by Swift, the Government assassin, who has Milton in his crosshairs and who is himself stabbed by Annabel who mistakes him for Milton. A third is punctured by an arrow shot by the glamorous assassin, also aimed at Milton. A fourth falls on Annabel, killing them both, while climbing around the outside of the hotel in an attempt to find Milton's room. (The team of Middle East fanatics are just carrying a medal they wish to award to Milton for all his good works.)

The real threat comes from Shelley, who intends selling the manuscript to the highest bidder. He holds Jeannie and Milton at gunpoint, having first killed the murderous publisher. Marty attempts to brain him with a vase, attracted from a shelf by his immense mental powers, but ends up pulling the bed – to which Magda has tied a naked Jeff – through the wall and sending it crashing into Shelley's back.

Milton finally gives his speech. His blockbuster 'exposé' is finally revealed to be a tired rehash of gossip, well-known fact and speculation. In the audience, Bulstrode and Lacey congratulate themselves on having evaded trouble.

> *Only fools will try to change the past,*
> *Retell the tale from first to last,*
> *The future is approaching fast,*
> *The present is a time we must not... wast.*

Charlie Higson had been determined to get his friend, *Fast Show* colleague and co-writer Paul Whitehouse into the series in some capacity. 'I was working on the series for two years,' he acknowledges, 'and I didn't want to not be working with Paul for all that amount of time. We work very well together, we enjoy working together. And I know when I write with him the writing comes out better. So I made sure I cast him in an episode and I made sure he wrote an episode with me. We were going to write another one together on the second series but he was too busy doing *Happiness* and *Jumpers for Goalposts*.'

Charlie's first-ever directing experience was, in a way, a reward for the time the series had taken away from his life. 'Basically I said, I'm going to be

working on this series for two years, including the writing, the producing and the post-production. Obviously I'm being paid a huge amount of money, but on top of that I would quite like to get some more out of it on a career front, would they let me direct one? And luckily they all said yes.'

Fortunately for Charlie and for the series, the experience was a positive one.

'We did it last, out of the six, so I'd been on set every day, I knew what we could shoot in a day, I knew what coverage you needed, I'd talked a lot to the editors… I'm not the kind of producer who sits in the office and does the sums. I probably should do that a bit more but I do like to be on set and be creatively involved.' He laughs. 'In the end, if you've got good people around you, they don't let you screw up.'

Musically, as well as humorously, the episode stands out from the rest of the season. The usual lush orchestral pieces and Britpop singles are edged out by a jazz-influenced sound.

'I wanted a very *Pink Panther* feel to that show,' Charlie admits, 'what with the load of assassins all trying to kill someone and ending up killing one another, so we did a lot of Henry Mancini-style big brass things on the soundtrack.'

The character names this time around are based, to a large extent, on historical British poets, with Shelley, Milton, Browning and Swift all turning up.

The episode showcases a number of familiar faces from a bewildering range of genres. Simon Day and Arabella Weir, both from *The Fast Show*, were cast as a murderous assassin and a murderous wife respectively, while Joanna Kanska (fondly remembered for her role in *A Very Peculiar Practice*) plays the murderous Magda. Simon Pegg, who appears alongside Jessica ('Felia') Stevenson in *Spaced*, is one of the Hammers of God assassins. Almost unrecognizable is Alexis Denisof (Wesley Wyndham-Price in the cult US series *Buffy the Vampire Slayer* and *Angel*) as a murderous security consultant. Charlie Higson explains how his casting came about.

'We'd written the part as American, and we ideally wanted an American to play it. We had a lot of English actors in who had varying success with the accent, but it needed to have that slightly cheesy, starry, American aura about the character, which Alexis has got. When we met him he did it in a cod Clint Eastwood way, which was very funny. I knew him vaguely because he went out with Caroline Aherne for a while.'

Most interesting casting, from the point of view of anybody who loved the original series, is that of Guy Pratt. Guy, the son of Mike Pratt, who originally played Jeff Randall back in the 1960s, plays the would-be assassin who manages to fry himself on an electric fence at the security conference. 'Guy was very pleased to get involved,' says Charlie. 'I think it was a fitting tribute to his dad.'

> How rare the secrets you would know,
> The secret places you could go,
> The secret paths both high and low,
> The secret spells that you could sow,
> And I these secrets can bestow,
> They shall be given unto… yeo.

Opposite: Swift (Simon Day), the rather stupid assassin, prepares to shoot Douglas Milton on the golf course.
Top: Douglas Milton and his wife Judith (Arabella Weir) have a quiet moment together. She has already hired an assassin to kill him.
Above: Mike Nicholson's storyboards of the scene where a member of the Hammers of God (played by Guy, the son of Mike Pratt) attempts to break through an electric fence.
Left: Richard Shelley (Alexis Denisof) makes a move on Jeannie.

a blast from the past

Written by Charlie Higson. Directed by Rachel Talalay

Some people retire to a little garden somewhere and grow roses for their last remaining days. Some people head out to see the world, taking chances they never did when they were younger. And some people just get bitter about the past, obsessing about the revenge they might take for real or imagined slights…

Somewhere round about thirty years ago, Marty Hopkirk's dad (Sergeant Larry Hopkirk) and his partner, Inspector Harry Wallis, attempted to arrest notorious gangster Sidney Crabbe. Crabbe shot Harry, wounding him, but fell to his death. Sidney's place in the criminal fraternity was taken by his brother Maurice, who started an affair with Harry Wallis's wife. During a confrontation between Larry Hopkirk, Harry Wallis and Maurice Crabbe, Larry Hopkirk was killed and Maurice plunged into a coma by a shot to the head.

Now, thirty years on, Harry Wallis walks into the offices of Randall & Hopkirk Security Services, and asks to see Marty. Jeff tells him that Marty is dead, and Harry explains that he is close to death himself. Sidney Crabbe's bullet has been working its way slowly toward his heart. He may only have a few days… a week or two at most. He wants to make amends for what happened in the past by using the proceeds from his insurance policies to makes sure that Maurice is kept comfortable – if he is still alive. Will Jeff find Maurice for him?

In Limbo, Marty has been allowed to mix with other spirits, but he is shocked when Sidney Crabbe turns up. Crabbe initially mistakes Marty for his father, and threatens to kill him. Again. When he discovers that Marty is his father's son, Sidney decides to kill him anyway.

Back on Earth, Marty manages to locate Maurice by entering 'cyberspace' through Jeff's computer. Jeff and Jeannie visit, and find him still in a coma, tended by a loving female companion – Harry Wallis's wife. They leave, having failed to persuade her to give out their location to Harry.

Harry Wallis, unwilling to take 'no' for an answer, forces Jeannie to drive him to the house where his wife and Maurice are located. He never wanted to give Maurice any money – he just wants to kill him in the last few days he has left.

Above: Vic Reeves shares a joke with Emilia Fox and Susan Brown during a break in filming.
Left: Larry Hopkirk (Vic Reeves) and Harry Wallis (Mark Benton) prepare to confront Maurice Crabbe, following his takeover of the family business.
Opposite top: Harry Wallis comforts his dying friend and colleague, not knowing that they would meet again after death.
Opposite right: In the Afterlife, there's plenty of time for leisure pursuits, and what better than fly fishing to pass the time away?

Jeff, alerted by Marty, sets off in pursuit. When they arrive, Harry attempts to kill Maurice but is attacked by the coma victim – he hasn't been in a coma at all, just pretending in order to shrug off the ghost of his brother Sidney. During the ensuing fracas, Jeff is shot and killed.

Sidney Crabbe appears on the scene and drags Marty off to the Pit of Oblivion, where souls are torn to pieces. Jeff's spirit comes to Marty's aid and pushes Sidney into the pit instead. Marty leads Jeff's spirit back to his body on Earth, refusing to let him die.

On Earth, Harry is still menacing his wife, Maurice and Jeannie with a gun. Marty reaches into his chest and nudges the bullet toward his heart. Harry dies, and not before time.

In Limbo, Harry is finally reunited with Larry Hopkirk – for a few seconds, until he is dragged screaming down to Hell…

In a perfect example of how things that seem completely seamless on television are anything but to the people who make the shows, the big song and dance number that Marty gets in 'A Blast from the Past' wasn't intended for Rachel Talalay's

episode at all, but rather was written for 'Paranoia', which Charlie Higson directed.

'Just before the big party sequence in "Paranoia", Charlie explains, 'Vic was going to enter the big, empty lecture hall, and there was just going to be a cleaner in there. He was getting upset because he'd seen Jeannie getting off with Shelley [the American security consultant], and so he went in and sang this ironic song about being in love with her. He was going to be arsing around on stage, and the spotlights were going to come on, and he was going to interfere with the cleaner with gusts of wind; but three things happened. Firstly I ran out of time, secondly, the way the sets worked out I was worried that we didn't have anywhere to properly stage it, and thirdly, Rachel's episode was about five minutes short, so in the end I asked if she wanted the song and dance routine in 'Blast from the Past' instead. At the time I thought my episode was going to be too long, but in the end I came in about four minutes too short as well.'

The highlight of the episode is, arguably, Vic's dual role as Marty and as his dad. While it might seem that playing Marty is easy and his dad is hard, Charlie believes that it's the other way around.

'I think it's quite difficult for Vic and Bob to play Randall & Hopkirk because I knew I was writing it for them and so I was writing it in versions of their Vic and Bob personas, which are obviously not them exactly but are kind of heightened versions of that. Vic found it a lot easier playing his dad because he could do a voice and have more of a disguise. The hardest part to play is something that is close to who you really are, because it's hard for you to suspend your own disbelief. I think it worked very well, with Marty meeting his dad, and I think we do believe they're two different people.'

Actor Dudley Sutton – Tinker in *Lovejoy*, and too many villains to name in various old ITC series – appears all-too-briefly as a lunatic old man.

'He was someone I really wanted to get in,' Charlie laments, 'but there weren't any other parts suitable. I feel that maybe we should get the character back, because he was such an iconic figure from all those old shows – and of course he was in the original *Randall & Hopkirk (Deceased).*'

In another attempt to link the old series and the new one, a cameo part was offered to actor Kenneth Cope, who originally played Marty Hopkirk. Although Cope declined to appear, Double Negative, the company behind the special effects, were able to lift a shot of Mike Pratt from the original series and place him into the episode set in limbo.

'That was a nice touch,' admits Higson. 'We'd found this one shot of Mike in a white suit from the original. In that particular episode he'd temporarily become a ghost like Marty. So in our episode five, when Marty gets his membership to the Limbo Club, there's a wide shot of all the ghosts hanging around in a bar. We used the shot of Mike just standing around talking in the background and it worked beautifully.'

Most of the episodes of this series have small touches that are worth looking out for. Here make sure you're watching as Harry Wallis arrives in the street outside Cope House, early on in the episode. He pushes the buzzer for the Randall & Hopkirk offices, but you can clearly see Marshall and Snellgrove marked underneath. They were

referred to briefly in 'Mental Apparition Disorder', and play a major part in, of course, 'Marshall and Snellgrove'. Also renting office space in the same building are Department S – the team whose job it was back in the 1960s ITC series of the same name to investigate bizarre and unusual goings on.

Also, when Marty's ghostly form is flitting through cyberspace looking for Maurice's whereabouts, various items of information flash past him – many of them related to his search. However, the name 'Captain Graves' can be seen, as can 'Radlands School'. Both appeared, of course, in the episode 'The Best Years of Your Death', which was also directed by Rachel Talalay. Also in there are buried references to Murray Gold and David Arnold (composers of the show's incidental music and theme respectively) and Greg Mitchell – a canine character from *The Smell of Reeves and Mortimer*.

> Onward and upwards, brave soul of mine,
> The horn blast calls you down the open road,
> Do you hear it?
> Do you see the golden sign?
> The heavens now are your abode,
> The purest air shall be your wine,
> And clouds of joy shall be your... fode.

Opposite left: *Sidney Crabbe's festering hatred of Larry Hopkirk has been burning inside him for years, and when Marty arrives in Limbo, Sidney (Paul Whitehouse) seizes his chance.*
Opposite right: *Harry and Larry, the old firm, together again in the Afterlife.*
Above: *Jeff helps Marty hurl Sidney into the Pit of Oblivion: as finally realized on screen and in storyboard form.*

a man of substance

Written by Charlie Higson, Directed by Mark Mylod

Living for ever. How many people can honestly say they wouldn't jump at the chance. And yet… watching everything around you turn to dust? Watching the world go mad? Watching the places you remember being buried under tarmac and concrete? Living for ever isn't enough; you have to be able to turn back the clock as well…

Lauren Dee, a beautiful *femme fatale* in a slinky red dress, hires Jeff to find her husband, who apparently disappeared in the vicinity of a village known as Hadell Wroxted. Jeff accepts the case, but has great difficulty finding the village, given that it fails to appear on any map. Eventually he locates it, and discovers it to be a quaint, Miss Marple locale that appears to be stuck in the 1950s. Or even earlier.

Jeff and Marty wander round the village, taking tea in the tea-rooms and drinks in the pub. The locals are affable enough, particularly Dickie Bechard, the publican, but there's something a little bit strange, a little bit off-kilter about them. And then Jeff realizes what it is – they can see Marty.

John Dee's name is registered in the pub guest book, but there's no other sign of him in the village. Marty tries to return to Limbo to discuss matters with Wyvern, but discovers that he can't leave the village. Equally, when Jeff tries to drive away he always ends up back in Hadell Wroxted.

Marty is seduced by Lauren Dee, who confides in him that the entire thing is a set-up. Her husband didn't disappear (or, rather, John Dee isn't her husband, although he did disappear). The villagers knew about Marty, and wanted him to help them, so Lauren was sent to lure him (by luring Jeff) to the village.

Right: Mrs Glauneck in the guise of 'Lauren Dee' (Jennifer Calvert) that she uses to lure Jeff and Marty to Hadell Wroxted.

Opposite top: Jeff and Marty outside the Hadell Wroxted Tea-rooms. If Dickie Bechard and his followers had their way, the world would be filled with similar tea-rooms.

Below: Mrs Glauneck (Elizabeth Spriggs) and PC Burns (Richard Riding).

Marty and Jeff are taken down into the (famous) Hadell Wroxted caves, where Dickie Bechard explains why they needed Marty. Six hundred years before, the country was being ravaged by the Black Death. Bechard led the villagers into the caves, and he and the local priest prayed to the Devil to deliver them from death. The Devil agreed, and since then the village has been held in between life and death, suspended between the real world and Limbo. What they needed was a ghost in a similar situation who was linked to a Chosen One on Earth – like Marty. By 'transubstantiating' Jeff, they can link themselves to Marty and thus gain their freedom. And ultimate power.

When Jeff asks what 'transubstantiation' means, he is told that the villagers are going to kill and eat him.

Marty appears to play along with this lunatic scheme, having been offered godhood by the villagers and seduced by his new-found ability to touch things and experience sensations again. Even Jeff's necessary death seems not to faze him.

Meanwhile, in Limbo, Wyvern is worrying about this turn of events. Transferring himself to Earth, he persuades Jeannie to travel to Hadell Wroxted, knowing that her appearance will cause Marty to feel guilty about what he is about to do.

As the villagers prepare the bonfire on which Jeff will be roasted, Marty begins to see that six hundred years of being suspended between life and death has set the villagers' opinions in stone. They wish to remake the world into their own peculiar image – an image of tea-rooms, no litter, no lager, dancing all day and communal singing all night. He refuses to go along with their plans at the last minute, and the villagers are sucked down into Hell.

Jeannie arrives, and can see Marty. With Wyvern's help, Marty smoothes her and Jeff's memory, so that neither of them will remember ever having seen him…

'A Man of Substance' was the last episode of series one to be shown, but the very first to be filmed.

'The reason,' Simon Wright explains, 'was that we had Reeves and Mortimer for the first time ever seriously in front of a film camera. And it was clear to us that we should not film the first episode until they'd settled down. Interestingly enough, when you actually look at the series you wouldn't guess that the first episode shot was the last episode shown.'

It's impossible, looking at the episode now, to see any signs that Vic and Bob are anything but natural actors. Charlie is content that the pair hit the ground running.

'One review got to episode six after having been very snotty about the series and about Vic and Bob, and said, "Oh, it's good to see they're finally settling into the roles." Well, no, it's that you're finally getting used to the style of the programme.'

One of the oddities of the episode is that Wyvern, for the first and last time that we see, leaves the realm of Limbo and appears on Earth.

'It was written before we'd come up with the idea of Wyvern,' Charlie confides, 'because he's not in the first episode either. I'd been thinking that it would be nice to show where Marty goes, and also there's the problem I saw in the original series that poor Kenneth Cope never got to act with anyone other than Mike Pratt, and because of the way they did the effects he wasn't even acting with him a lot of the time. I thought it was very limited, and limiting, when Vic can be so very funny when he's with other people, to have the whole series with Vic just talking to Bob. And Bob said, "Can we have a kind of Obi-Wan Kenobi figure, a mystical spirit guide who could teach Marty what to do?" So those ideas all came together, and I had to then go back and work out how I was going to get him into episode six. I'd wanted it to be that when they were in the village they were trapped, and if Marty could keep on popping backwards and forwards we lost that idea. So we decided that Wyvern could see what was going on and had to come down and

Above: *One of June Nevin's designs for a woodland nymph.*
Top: *The famous Hadell Wroxted caves were actually filmed in Chislehurst in Kent.*
Opposite top: *Marty interrupts a saucy game.*
Opposite bottom: *Even the local vicar (Richard Durden) was party to Dickie Bechard's deal with the Devil.*

Above: Uneasy lies the head that wears the crown.
Right: Dickie Bechard (Gareth Thomas) bears an uncanny similarity to his ancestor on the pub sign.
Opposite: The destruction of Hadell Wroxted and the climactic moments of the episode, both in storyboard form and as they were finally realized on screen.

intervene because the implications of what was going on were too huge.'

If there's one thing about the episode that troubles Charlie Higson, it's the discrepancy between what he envisioned and what was finally achieved. 'We didn't have a budget for prosthetics and special masks,' he laments, 'so there were a lot more demons and weird characters in the original scripts that we had to drop.'

What used up the budget was the spectacular last moments of the episode.

'There was one shot there that took eight months to do,' Charlie sighs. 'It was the shot of the village going up in the whirlwind and being sucked down into the hole. It was the first one we shot, so Double Negative started working on it then, and it was one of the last shots to be delivered... But they do like to do things properly.'

As a reflection of the generally hellish nature of the plot, the names of many of the characters are those of demons from esoteric writings, all apart from Lauren Dee. She (or, more precisely, her missing 'husband' John) is a reference to Doctor John Dee, Queen Elizabeth I's alchemist and astrologer.

For long-term fans of the SF and fantasy genres, it was nice to see Gareth Thomas appearing as the local publican and architect of the village's preservation. Thomas, who may never escape the shadow of *Blake's Seven*, in which he played the eponymous hero, had a ball playing the part.

'It was fun,' he says. 'I enjoyed it enormously. I have to confess that Reeves and Mortimer are...' he pauses for effect, '... lovely guys. And I had a chance to work with Liz Spriggs, whom I hadn't seen for twenty years or more since we were at the Royal Shakespeare Company, and now the pair of us were doing this bizarre thing. But it was great. Wonderful.'

For a Shakespearian actor who takes his craft seriously, being placed alongside two anarchic comedians might have created problems, but Gareth Thomas has nothing but praise for the duo.

'To their eternal credit, the pair of them had respect. In the sense that we were actors – not just guests or personalities – they had enormous respect for that.'

The episode – indeed, the first series – ends on a note that puzzled fans at the time, hinting as it does that the ghost and his partner had separated for ever. Simon Wright is unrepentant.

'At the end of series one, Randall & Hopkirk are divorced from each other in perpetuity. Why did we do that? Because we wanted people to feel very sad. I think it's a really touching moment. I don't think people always get it, but perhaps if they watch it again you realize that Jeff's memory is erased, Marty is dead, and the last six hours of adventure are over. We did it for dramatic effect, and just in case the series never did come back.'

c/u on Jeff's tied hands ...

Jeannie reacts ...

...low angle of J.&J.

...Tight two-shot of J.&J.

"Duck!"

Low angle of J.&J. "Let's get ..."

Ext. Overlooking village Sc. 65

The pit sucks the village away

..."only peaceful countryside remains."

Jeff: "What's going on?"

..."the ghostly figure ..." J.&J. turn and leave frame.

Marty follows as car is ejected ...

whatever possessed you

Written by Charlie Higson and Gareth Roberts. Directed by Metin Huseyin

Above: *Marty returns from Limbo to help Jeff again, and has to remind Jeff of who he is.* **Opposite:** *Jeannie, her body possessed by the spirit of Sonia Cronenberg, attempts to seduce Jeff so that her lover can take over his body.*

They say you can never go back. The also say that love lasts for ever. Sometimes, however, if the love is strong enough, you can go back. The problem is, how do you ever get out?

The Traveller's Halt, a fine old house converted into a hotel, is having problems. Not the usual kind of problems – unpleasant guests, rattling plumbing, *Star Trek* conventions – but rather a series of deaths in which the victims are burned to a crisp while leaving their surroundings untouched. Jeff and Jeannie are hired to find out what's happening, just as a party of ghost hunters book in, hoping to catch sight of one of the hotel's noted regular phenomena – the Burning Man or the Faceless Woman.

Shortly after booking into her room, Jeannie is possessed by the spirit of a previous guest – Sonia Cronenberg. Sonia burned to death in the hotel in 1951 with her lover, Captain James Romero, after the two of them killed her husband, but their spirits have become trapped there, not ghosts but not alive, somewhere in-between.

The possessed Jeannie seduces Jeff as part of her plan for herself and Romero (who is present only as a burning male figure) to completely take over Jeannie and Jeff's bodies. The plan involves recreating the exact circumstances under which the two of them died, which involved an accident with a glass of flaming liqueur. Marty realizes what is happening and attempts to stop it, but he is stymied when the ghost hunters attempt an impromptu exorcism.

Sonia's plan comes within a hair's breadth of working, but Marty has pulled a bit of a fast one. He takes over Jeff's body, carrying Jeff and Jeannie's spirits with him. With her lover now finally, irretrievably dead and her spirit removed from the hotel that has had her trapped, Sonia too finally goes to her rest.

'Whatever Possessed You' kicks off series two in fine style, tying up all the loose ends left over from the end of season one and setting the series firmly on a darker, more character-driven path. Despite its appearance of solidity, however, it was assembled from two different scripts, one written by Charlie Higson and one by Gareth Roberts, a young writer whose credits range from novelizations of other television programmes (*Cracker*) through original novels based on other television programmes (*Doctor Who*) to a solid body of scripting and script-editing work on soap opera (*Coronation Street*, *Brookside* and *Emmerdale*).

Gareth recalls, 'Charlie had written the opening episode to the second series, which was about a film crew going to a haunted house to do a kind of *Ghostwatch* type programme. Basically they were going to set up cameras to see if this place was as haunted as everyone said it was – and it was. They'd been planning to fake it but they didn't need to in the end, because there actually were ghosts.'

Gareth had already written the episode 'Pain Killers' for series two, and Charlie was impressed enough with his writing that he asked him to write a second script. As with the first, Charlie supplied a one-line idea and Gareth fleshed it out to sixty-odd pages of scenes, characters and dialogue. This time, however, things didn't quite go to plan.

'The brief I got for that one was "Jeannie is possessed", and that was it,' Gareth explains. 'I thought what it would be quite nice to do – because the character Millie [Fox] plays is a very modern woman – would be to make her a kind of Ruth Ellis character, because she's got that kind of blonde bombshell look about her. I think the feedback from the first series was that she wanted to do more interesting and varied things, so I just came up with the idea of the red lips and the big red dress and took it from there. And that tied in with the idea of it being a haunted house with a trapped spirit.'

The idea of a ghost based on Ruth Ellis must have been appealing to everyone involved with the

'Oh, no, look! It's the trouser press – of terror! And there! It's the complimentary biscuits – of death!'

Jeff

production. Ellis was the last woman to be hanged in Britain, having been convicted in 1955 of shooting her boyfriend, a racing driver. Her image was further inflated by the 1985 film *Dance with a Stranger*, where the part of Ellis was played by Miranda Richardson. The contrast between this forceful, glamorous woman and the repressed 1950s milieu was key to both the film and Gareth's script. 'It's the kind of era we don't really see on television or films,' he points out, 'because it's so drab and unpleasant.'

With the two scripts already written – Charlie's 'television crew in a haunted house' and Gareth's

Above: The ghost-hunters come to the Traveller's Halt.
Bottom: James Whale (Hywel Bennett) doesn't believe in ghosts when he first arrives at the Traveller's Halt. By the time he leaves, he is a ghost.
Opposite top: John Thomson plays a guest whose stay is brought to a fiery close.
Opposite bottom: The hotel maid is taken over by Sonia Cronenberg.

'1950s vamp possesses Jeannie' – things started to go in an unexpected direction.

Simon Wright remembers that Charlie's original episode had been deliberately written to explain how the duo got back together after Jeff's memory was erased in 'A Man of Substance' and Marty ascended to Heaven for good. 'Charlie was very concerned that we address this matter at the beginning of series two,' he explains. 'Vic and Bob's view was that a lot of people wouldn't even have

got the fact that Jeff's memory was erased at the end of series one, but Charlie's first episode of series two – as he wrote it – was very much about getting them back together. We all felt that Gareth Roberts's episode – which pretty much ignored that – was better in narrative terms because we didn't have the same problems of set-up. So the solution was to put them together. We pulled back on the drama of them re-meeting while recognizing that they had to re-meet.'

'Charlie and I sat down and re-storylined it together,' Gareth adds, 'and then Charlie took it away and clicked and dragged, and put the whole thing together.'

The final product – the amalgamation of scripts by two different writers – is a smooth and spooky ghost story set in a hotel in two different periods of time. One suspects that lurking in the minds of both writers was the old ITV series *Sapphire and Steel*, which starred Joanna Lumley and David McCallum as detectives who stuck time back together again when it became unstuck. One story in particular had the two heroes skipping back and forth between the 1930s and the 1970s in an old manor house. The manor house in *Sapphire and Steel* was accomplished entirely in the television studio; *Randall & Hopkirk (Deceased)*, with slightly more money and slightly more time to play with, filmed their dual-time-zone hotel on location. But not in an actual hotel.

'The interiors were done at this very, very spooky Doctor Barnardo's home near Watford, which has been closed for years,' Gareth recalls. 'They'd just been doing the television series *Band of Brothers* there, and we actually used a bit of their set. It was incredible: it was a freezing, abandoned building in the middle of Hertfordshire in the middle of November, but there were all kinds of tricks with light played to make it look warm and comfortable. Obviously the crew could wear what they wanted to, but Millie was in a strapless dress and between takes she was wrapped in a big pac-a-mac with a three-bar fire at her feet. I went for a wander around the rest of the building and it was

just the spookiest place I've ever been in my life. But a very good location.'

Gareth had assumed that, given the right location, the effect of moving back and forth in time would be very simple to accomplish. He was wrong. 'I thought when I was writing "Whatever Possessed You" that it was a very economical, very cheap episode to do,' he says. 'I very deliberately set it all in the one location, very few sets, and the only effect was the going back from 2001 to 1951, which I thought would just be a simple matter of re-dressing the sets. But it was just a terrible headache for the crew. They had to be in there at five o'clock in the morning changing everything to do the different time zones, so it was actually much more expensive than I would have thought.'

Production Designer Simon Waters, however, enjoyed the process of dressing the location, despite the headaches.

'There's a very strong colour theme for each room,' he enthuses, 'because you need to know whose room you're in. When you read the story it's so complicated, so the design has to help tell the story. I made Jeff's room deep red – the pictures were red, the carpets were red, the bedcovers – and Jeannie's room was green, and Room 308 was gold. I kept the colour scheme the same when we did the flashbacks. I said to the set decorator that everything in Jeannie's room had to be green. We didn't divert from the green at all. That's quite fun, because it makes it quite stylized.'

Both of Gareth's scripts for the series contain references to other television shows or films, but in 'Whatever Possessed You' it was Charlie Higson who put them in. All of the characters in the episode are named after horror-film directors – horror films being a particular love of Higson's. Those people who care about these things may wish to look out for: Mr Browning (Tod Browning, director of the original *Dracula*); Virginia Carpenter (John Carpenter, of *The Fog* and *The Thing* fame); Hettie Craven (Wes Craven, creator of Freddie Kruger and the *Nightmare on Elm Street* series); Sonia Cronenberg (David Cronenberg, best

Above: *Sonia Cronenberg possesses Jeannie's body and forces Jeannie to kiss Jeff – not that it takes much forcing.* **Opposite top:** *Wyvern has interests in this case that even Marty doesn't realize.* **Opposite bottom:** *James Romero and Sonia Cronenberg, the star-crossed lovers whose efforts to regain the life they once had lead to so many other deaths.*

known film for *The Fly*); Miss Hooper (*The Texas Chainsaw Massacre*'s Tobe Hooper); Mr Lewton (Val Lewton, producer of the classic *Cat People*); James Romero (George Romero, director of *Night of the Living Dead*); and Roger Whale (James Whale, the humorist who gave us *Frankenstein* and *The Bride of Frankenstein*).

Director Metin Huseyin had been brought onto the series following the departure of Mark Mylod (to direct the *Ali G* movie) and Rachel Talalay (to have a baby).

'I'd worked with Metin years before on a Harry Enfield special,' Charlie says. 'He'd done a lot of comedy work early in his career, and then gone on to solid drama like *Common as Muck* and *Tom Jones*. He'd also recently done a film – *It Was an Accident*.'

'Each director has different strengths,' Simon Wright adds, 'and Metin's is basic narrative skills. He's done a lot of television and he really knows how to tell a story. He's very much a performance director and he has a very clear eye on where the plot is going at any given moment. And what you have in Metin's episodes, as a result, are very successful, well-told plots.'

Watch out for actor Hywel Bennett as Roger Whale, the journalist at the end of his tether. Bennett was a cherub-faced actor in the 1970s, appearing with Alec Guinness in the seminal spy thriller *Tinker Tailor Soldier Spy* and playing the eponymous hero of the sitcom *Shelley*. Watch out also for John Thomson, one of Charlie Higson's *Fast Show* colleagues, as an unlucky hotel guest, and well-known actress Nichola McAuliffe (*Surgical Spirit*) as the ghostly Virginia Carpenter.

Remember this, dear friend, from all mankind
I was allowed to choose,
Such joy, I know you felt, when you first heard the news,
But wait, what would befall us if our bond we were to lose?
That question is not one that we should ever want to... pooze.

Wyvern: 'Are you thinking what I'm thinking, Marty?'

Marty: 'I don't know. Were you thinking about anti-barnacle paint?'

revenge of the bog people

Written by Charlie Higson and Kate Woods. Directed by Charlie Higson

Old girlfriends… old boyfriends… who hasn't wondered how things might have gone if arguments hadn't happened? Most of us never get the chance to find out, but some bonds survive even death…

Jeff knocks himself out in the office one night, and is discovered next day by Jeannie. She rushes him to hospital, where he meets Freya Cargill – his former fiancée. Freya left him ten years ago when he tried, and failed, to find out what had happened to her missing father. The general assumption was that Andrew Cargill – an expert on Iron Age Britain – had been stealing relics from the museum where he worked and, having made enough money, had absconded. Freya disagreed – she thought he had been murdered.

Now Freya wants Jeff to investigate her father's disappearance again. Jeff, too besotted by love to be thinking rationally, doesn't wonder why she is suddenly interested again after ten years. Or why she dresses always in white. Or why she won't let him touch her.

Marty does. Marty knows that Freya is dead.

Not that Marty can do much to warn Jeff. No, he's got too much on his hands already, watching

Below: Boudicca (Celia Imrie) and Maximus (Mark Williams) share an intimate but historically suspect moment.
Opposite: Caradoc Evans (Freddie Jones) shares his knowledge. Scenes in the original script showed that he had become a teacher after leaving the museum.

over Nesbit – another of Wyvern's students who is, apparently, a bit 'wayward'. It's Marty's job to straighten him out a bit, but it seems to be working the other way around: Nesbit is leading Marty astray.

Jeff and Jeannie talk to Professors Doleman and McKern – former colleagues of Andrew Cargill – but they can shed no light on the by-now-ancient mystery of his disappearance. They are more concerned with boxing up one of the museum's bog people, a preserved Iron Age corpse which is being sent to Denmark for an exhibition.

Stymied in his attempts to check Cargill's locker by McKern and Doleman, Jeff hides in the museum and sneaks a peek after it closes. He finds a sheet of paper covered in runes which has fallen down the side of the locker.

Caradoc Evans, another old colleague of Cargill's, translates the runes into an allusive accusation of betrayal. This turns Jeff's thoughts back to McKern and Doleman. He returns to the museum and discovers that the preserved Iron Age body is actually of more recent origin – it's Freya's father, recognizable by the birthmark on his hand.

Doleman and McKern confront Jeff, admitting that they had been stealing relics from the museum to fund their eventual retirement. When Cargill discovered them, they killed him. They are about to kill Jeff when Jeannie (and her sister Wendy) interfere. There is a fight, evil is punished, good is rewarded.

In a final meeting, Jeff discovers that Freya is dead, and achieves some kind of closure.

The script for 'Revenge of the Bog People' went through numerous changes between initial conception and final draft, illustrating just how problematic television can be.

'When we were doing the second series,' Charlie Higson explains, 'I commissioned a lot more scripts than I actually needed – I had a couple of other writers doing stuff as well. Kate, who was a new writer recommended to me by another production company, wrote two scripts, one of

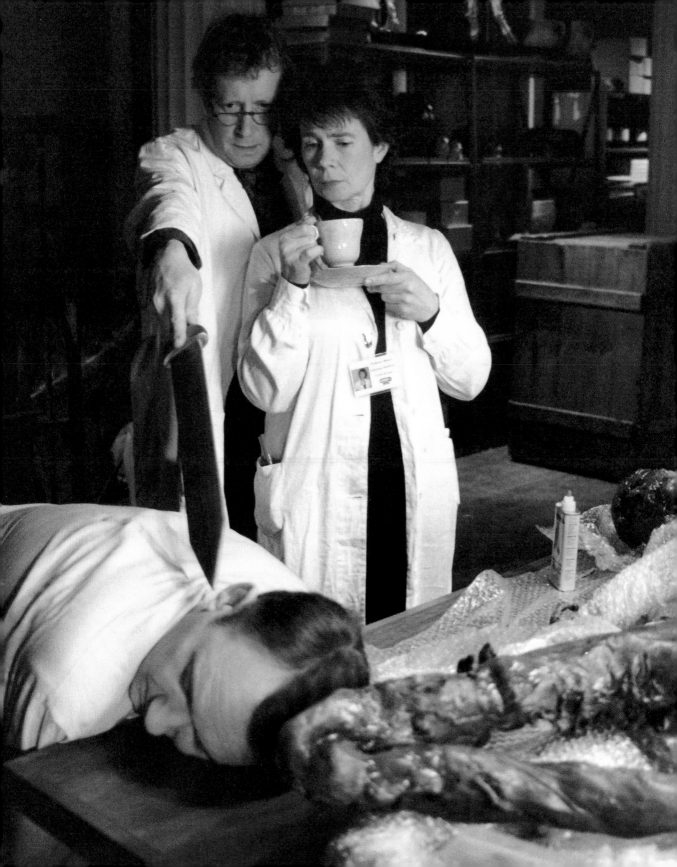

which we decided not to do because we had too many. The other one was a *Sixth Sense* kind of thing where another ghost was involved who we didn't know was a ghost, and it was an old girlfriend of Jeff's, which was an idea that I loved. And from a list that I had of little worlds to go into, Kate was very keen on the museum side of things.'

At this point, the intention was firmly that Kate should write the entire episode by herself.

'So she went off,' Charlie continues, 'and came up with a script where the relationship stuff with the ghost was fantastic – it was all lovely stuff. The mechanics of the rest of the plot were interesting, but obviously the detective side of things wasn't the area she had been particularly interested in. She had written it about a bunch of Egyptologists, and the plot was about smuggling drugs within mummies. I felt the whole Egyptology area had been slightly done to death, in the horror area and the comedy horror area – with things like *The Mummy* and *Stargate*. I'd always been fascinated by bog people, and they're a bit more British, so I kept the basic structure of her plot, I kept the ghost, I changed the mummies to bog people and changed the motivation for the actual crime. And I introduced slightly more detective elements into it, although it's not exactly Sherlock Holmes.'

Despite his amendments and additions to Kate's script, Charlie still remains impressed with what she accomplished.

'Certainly she wrote some lovely scenes with the ghost,' he agrees. 'The big change I made on that front was that, in Kate's version, we don't realize that the woman's a ghost until the very end. I thought that was a bit *Sixth Sense*, and I thought that people would probably be ahead of us on that, and you run up against the problem that the character always has to wear white. So we did a kind of *Vertigo* thing on it, where the audience knows before the central character who this mystery woman really is. Which gives it more of a sense of tragedy and irony for Jeff, because we see him doggedly going on hoping everything is going to turn out right, yet we know that it never can.'

The location in which filming for the episode took place had to be carefully chosen to look like an ornate, classical museum. And there aren't that many of those around.

'We found a location, because we knew we couldn't afford to build anything,' Production Designer Simon Waters admits. 'The British Museum was prohibitively expensive, but we found a beautiful room at Syon House in Isleworth, and then had a few carefully placed sarcophagi to give it atmosphere.'

Despite Charlie Higson's concerns over the Egyptology quotient of the original script, those sarcophagi had originally been constructed for the Hollywood blockbuster *The Mummy*. 'We had

Above: *Jeff meets his old flame, Freya Cargill (Anna Wilson-Jones) in a squash club – which is handy, as she only ever wears white.*
Opposite: *Professors Doleman and McKern (Mark Williams and Celia Imrie), discuss the fate of Jeff, the professional nosy parker.*

four sarcophagi and various sphinxes,' Simon admits, rather sheepishly.

The room itself, ideal though it was in some ways, had to be significantly altered in order to make it suitable.

'I sold Charlie on the idea of this huge room with a floodlit table in the middle,' Simon says, 'and all the action can happen around the table, on which are all the elements for the fight – Iron Age swords and so on.'

Despite Simon Waters's detailed proposals, Charlie Higson had some of his own ideas.

'Charlie had the idea of having a Viking boat there. I said, "You don't just get a Viking boat", but actually I thought it was a nice idea, because it was something the characters could interact with, something they could smash during the fight. We went to a hire company, and I got a 1950s rowing boat from them for free, and turned it into a Viking boat with a bit of plaster and black paint and a burner. I made the ends skeletal and put lots of clamps all over it, so it looked as if they were reconstructing it.'

The boat wasn't all Charlie wanted. Not by a long chalk.

'And then he wanted a skeleton. He didn't mean a sparrow, he meant a pterodactyl. That would cost megabucks. But I knew he wanted it for the fight, and it's not my job to turn around and simply answer "We haven't got the money", because no one wants to hear that. So I built a wire frame and got a polystyrene carver to do the backbone, then we rang the British Museum. They have moulds of their dinosaurs, so they ran us off some plaster casts of some tibias and a big jaw with teeth. We got a big thigh bone and a skull, and I put the skull on a wire armature and wired up the rest of the bones, and the illusion was created.'

The fight scene takes its toll on the skeleton and, like the world's largest jigsaw puzzle, it ends up in pieces on the floor.

'I said, "If it's going to collapse it won't go back together,"' Simon points out, 'and Charlie said,

Right: *Nesbit (Matt Lucas) and Marty look on powerlessly (literally) as…*
Below: *…Jeff and Professor Doleman cross swords.*
Opposite top: *Marty Hopkirk, looking like the back end of a surrealist horse, as he waits to appear in Jeff's nightmares.*
Opposite bottom: *Filming the DIY dream sequence in which Marty and Nesbit try to warn Jeff about Freya. In this scene Nesbit impersonates Jeannie while Marty impersonates Freya.*

"That's okay, we'll do it in one take. We'll roll two cameras on it."'

This episode showcases a number of familiar faces: Mark Williams, who plays Professor Doleman, is an old *Fast Show* alumnus, whereas Freddie Jones (Caradoc Evans) and Celia Imrie are both fine character actors who are known for their slightly comic, slightly grotesque creations. Freddie Jones is one of the few actors, by the way, who has appeared in both the original *Randall & Hopkirk (Deceased)* and the new version. Matt Lucas, who plays George Daws on Vic and Bob's game show with a difference, *Shooting Stars*, appears as the mischievous sprite Nesbit.

Charlie Higson's hand can be seen in the character names, which are almost without exception the names of actors who played the part of Number Two in the cult 1960s television series *The Prisoner*. Watch out for: Freya Cargill (Patrick Cargill); Professor Doleman (Guy Doleman); Professor McKern (Leo McKern) and Caradoc Evans (Clifford Evans).

o happy isle

Written by Charlie Higson.
Directed by Metin Huseyin

Discrimination is all about making distinctions between people and then treating them differently because of those distinctions. But what if the barriers were blurred? What if 'we' were suddenly 'they', and vice versa? Would the world be a better place?

Arriving on a small island off the coast of Scotland, Jeff and Jeannie set to work investigating the apparent suicide of a lad who worked at the local brewery, but find themselves stymied by the close-mouthed populace. The lad in question was a computer programmer from the mainland, brought in to cure some kind of problem with the brewery's computers, and it would appear that he was being ostracized because he was gay.

Opposite top: *The exterior shots for the island were filmed at Clovelly harbour, in north Devon.*
Opposite bottom: *The locals (Gerald Lepkowski, Charlie Higson and Ford Kiernan) promise a warm welcome.*
Right: *The slightly strange landlady and landlord, The Commodore (Glynis Brooks) and Babbacombe (Rupert Vansittart).*
Below: *Jeff and Jeannie escape from jail.*

The island is run on almost medieval lines, with the local Laird – Berry Pomeroy – having almost complete power over the inhabitants. He owns all the property, he conducts the post-mortems on anyone who dies and he dispenses justice in accordance with ancient rules. Marty discovers that he also has a hidden laboratory beneath his castle staffed by Japanese scientists. They appear to be working on a serum code-named Tiresias.

During their investigations, Jeff and Jeannie pick up hints that something is changing amongst the population. The butch fishermen and brewery employees begin to display a softer, more feminine side, men are seen holding hands in the street and the local police chief declares his love for Jeff. Even Jeannie succumbs to the odd influence, and finds herself as attracted to Jeff as the police chief.

Jeannie and Jeff are arrested to keep them from pursuing their investigations, but with Marty's help they break out of jail and make their way to the Laird's castle. During a tense confrontation, they discover his secret plan: to contaminate the beer exported from the island with Tiresias 28 – a synthetic hormone that suppresses masculine instincts. Concerned at the damage mankind is doing to the environment, Pomeroy intends calling a halt to the entire human race, stopping them from breeding without actually killing anyone.

Marty's newly discovered ability to smash glass objects by singing high notes when jealous comes in handy, as he manages to break the vat containing the Tiresias 28 (but only when he forces Jeff to kiss Jeannie). Pomeroy dies, poisoned by the flood of pure Tiresias 28, and Jeff and Jeannie leave for the mainland. One suspects, however, that the island will never be the same again.

LAB AREA

Charlie Higson's most outlandish script for series two of *Randall & Hopkirk (Deceased)* looks slightly further afield than old ITC series for its sources. There's a very obvious – and fully acknowledged – debt to the cult 1973 British film classic *The Wicker Man*, of course, in which a policeman sent from the mainland to a small Scottish island discovers that the Laird has revived the old pagan traditions, and eventually finds himself sacrificed by the locals to ensure a good harvest. Ally that with an episode of the 1970s ecological thriller series *Doomwatch* called 'The Battery People' in which hard-bitten miners become effeminate as a result of synthetic hormones accidentally getting into their bodies, and you might come up with something approaching 'O Happy Isle'.

The original idea for 'O Happy Isle' had been suggested by Vic Reeves and Bob Mortimer during series one. They wanted Charlie Higson to write a script in which a villain tries to turn everyone in the world gay. It's the kind of idea that

might work as a five-minute sketch on *Vic and Bob's Big Night Out*, but expanding it to fifty minutes without losing the audience had to be handled carefully if it wasn't going to cause offence.

Simon Wright, for one, is very happy with the final result.

'The whole concept behind "O Happy Isle", I think, is hysterical,' he says. 'We were worried about it in terms of taste and decency, and the BBC were very worried about it. They thought that we might get a reaction from the anti-gay lobby. None of us ever worried about it being offensive to gays: we were worried about it being offensive to middle-England. Metin directed that episode and he did, probably rightly, pull it back so that the campiness is quite natural and quite tender and warm between the men.'

'I thought,' Charlie Higson explains, 'that one way to get round the idea of it looking anti-gay would be to set it on an island like the Isle of Man where it's illegal to be gay. I thought that would

Right: The drug that Berry Pomeroy has placed in the island's beer begins to have its effect on the locals.
Below: Jeannie develops a taste for the local Iron Man lager.
Opposite: Marty wonders about Jeff's hat.

defuse the situation. Of course, that actually made it more complicated as far as the BBC were concerned. So I had to go in a roundabout way in order not to offend anybody – inventing a local term for gay and so on.'

Familiar faces include comedy actor and improvisational genius John Sessions, playing Combe Fishacre, and veteran film and television actor George Baker, who adds a touch of class to proceedings in the role of Berry Pomeroy. Baker, who was a matinee idol of sorts back in the 1950s, is best known these days for his recurring role as Chief Inspector Wexford in the television adaptations of Ruth Rendell's detective novels.

Their characters – like many others in the script – are named for some of the towns and villages within a small area of Devon. 'The location team realized,' Charlie recalls, 'because they were down there scouting for places to shoot, and they suddenly realized everywhere they looked was a character in the show.'

Above left: Berry Pomeroy (George Baker) illustrates with his shotgun what the islanders will be losing if they drink the local beer.

Above: A storyboard sequence showing Pomeroy's ultimate and ironic fate.

Left: Chief Inspector Woodhuish (Paul Young) harbours secret desires for Jeff.

Opposite top: Jeff tries to make Marty jealous.

Opposite bottom: John Sessions as Combe Fishacre, boss of the island's brewery.

marshall & snellgrove

Written by Charlie Higson. Directed by Metin Huseyin

Double bluffs. Triple bluffs. Games within games. Smoke and mirrors. Sometimes it's hard, being a simple detective in a complicated world…

Jeff and Jeannie are hired by Meredith Hortweldine to protect him from his twin brother Jasper. Meredith and Jasper are the sons of Sir Leslie Hortweldine, who made his fortune inventing freezer technology before his recent death in a freezer of his own making. Sir Leslie's millions are to be divided between Meredith and Jasper, but each hates the other and Meredith believes his life is in danger.

Interestingly enough, Jasper has already hired

Above: *Jeannie and Charlie Marshall (Shaun Parkes).*
Right: *Jeannie and Jeff, along with their client Meredith Hortweldine (John Dougall).*
Opposite: *Marshall and Snellgrove (not yet Deceased).*

Charlie Marshall and Sebastian Snellgrove, the detectives whose offices are directly beneath Jeannie and Jeff, to protect his life.

The four detectives meet up on the steps of the Hortweldine twins' house as they start their respective bodyguarding duties. The house has been split in two, with each brother occupying a half to himself. The halves are decorated in wildly different styles; Meredith's is fusty and Victorian, matching the man himself, while Jasper's is funky and psychedelic.

Mrs Proffitt, the solicitor acting for the Hortweldine family, arrives to obtain signatures on the paperwork. Once that has been done, the money will be transferred and the brothers will go their separate ways.

Meredith Hortweldine, now a very rich man, leaves with Jeannie for the airport, just as an explosion rips through the house. It's apparently due to a leaky gas main, and it kills Jasper Hortweldine (and Sebastian Snellgrove, who had stayed in the house to check something suspicious).

Something is obviously amiss, but the detectives aren't quite sure what it is. Firstly they suspect that Jasper had attempted to kill Meredith with a faked gas explosion in order to get Meredith's half of the money but had blown himself up with his own bomb. Then they suspect that Meredith had already killed Jasper and was impersonating his brother in order to obtain all the money, but then Meredith himself dies in a plane crash, scuppering that theory. Then they suspect a previously unknown illegitimate brother – Anthony – but they have no proof. Then they suspect the solicitor, Celia Proffitt, but she apparently kills herself. It's a tangled web – one only resolved when Jeff remembers that Sir Leslie Hortweldine gained his money through freezer technology, and when Marty discovers that Anthony is a make-up artist. Meredith, Jasper and Celia Proffitt were all dead before the case started. Anthony had killed them all, then killed Sir Leslie, but he had to pretend to be Meredith, Jasper and

Celia in order to obtain the money. Once that had happened he could cheerfully get their bodies out of cold storage and fake their deaths.

Charlie and Jeff reveal Anthony's plan, and Sebastian Snellgrove, who has been hanging around with Marty, can ascend to Heaven in peace.

The unlikely presence of another detective agency directly underneath the offices of Jeff Randall and Marty Hopkirk was set up in series one. The nameplate outside the front door of Cope House lists Marshall and Snellgrove as occupants, and the cleaner mentions having 'done' for them. The roots go further back than that, however, as Charlie Higson explains.

'It was a nod to the original series. Kenneth Cope said that when they started working on it, he and Mike Pratt could never remember what they were called. Their joke was that they called themselves Marshall and Snellgrove, which was actually the name of a department store. I thought that was a nice little idea to weave into the series. Once I'd had this idea of Marshall and Snellgrove being downstairs I thought it would be great to do an episode with a pair of rival detectives who were working on the same case but from the other side. It was a mirror image to what had happened with Randall & Hopkirk.'

A mirror image which was then worked into the entire structure of the episode, what with the twins who supposedly hire the two teams of detectives and the house which is itself a mirror image, with each twin living in a separate half.

The set design, unsurprisingly, required some creative ingenuity to film.

'The idea was that the twins had identical houses, side by side,' Production Designer Simon Waters explains, 'so each is a mirror image of the other – one is *circa* 1960 and the other one is kind of Dickensian. So it's like having two terraced houses together, but without the wall in between. That was what we were looking for. We looked at loads of locations and it just didn't happen. We

got to the stage where we were only about three weeks away from filming and we still hadn't got a location.'

At that point, with so much money and so many people depending on a decision, panic started to set in.

'So we all sat down – me, Metin, Charlie – and we went back through everything we had found, everything we had seen. I don't know if it was Metin's idea or Charlie's to shoot on the location we liked the best, to dress it all for one of the twins and then have a four-day break while we revamped the house *circa* 1960, and then flip the film in the camera, but that's what we did.'

As is true of so many things in life, the solution to one problem just produces others.

'When you flip the film everything goes backwards,' Simon Waters continues. 'We couldn't have any writing, because that would be in reverse. The biggest problem, of course, was costumes, because buttons go the other side, and partings are terrible. If you have a centre parting,

Above: *Marshall and Snellgrove appear to be doing rather better than Randall & Hopkirk ever did. Perhaps they intercept potential clients on their way up the stairs…*
To evoke the feeling of back projection (as used in the original series), *all the driving sequences are shot in a studio and the background film, and reflections, are added later by Double Negative.*
Bottom: *Jasper Hortweldine shows his new bodyguards around the house – his side of* the house, at any rate.
Opposite: *A stairway in Meredith and Jasper's house – the stairs would be filmed one way for one side of the house, then redressed and filmed in reverse for the other side.*

it's fine, but if you have a parting on one side then it appears on the other side, and people's faces look very unnatural if they've been reversed.' '

'That gave us problems,' Charlie Higson points out, 'because all the actors' clothing had to be exactly symmetrical, which is why Millie has a slightly bizarre hairstyle. It was her idea of a symmetrical hairstyle.'

'We did have one room that we split, and we dressed half and half,' says Simon Waters. 'I had a white shagpile carpet on one side and old floorboards on the other, and that made a very clear division. An actor could walk from one half to the other half. And that was a shot they didn't get. It's a shame... in the final cut it looks like they're completely different locations.'

It may be worth pointing out, for those people who hadn't realized, that actor John Dougall plays five different roles in this episode.

Left top and bottom: The many faces of actor John Dougall.
Below: Jeff also gets to don a disguise.
Above: Charlie Marshall (Shaun Parkes) wonders why he always ends up doing the paperwork while his partner spends the money.
Opposite: When Sebastian Snellgrove (Colin McFarlane) was alive, he couldn't see Marty. When he was dead, he couldn't see enough of him.

pain killers

Written by Gareth Roberts. Directed by Charlie Higson

Below: *Jeff in the clutches of Colonel Anger's men.*
Opposite: *Sir Derek Jacobi as Colonel Anger, kept alive by strange drugs.*

Pain is good. Pain is our friend. Pain warns us when something bad is happening to us. And so delaying pain, stopping its messages from getting through, that would be bad. Wouldn't it?

Jeff and Jeannie are hired by representatives of a sinister Government department to investigate The Pain Corporation. It's a secretive private firm carrying out research on the frontiers of science, but there are rumours that things inside are way out of whack. Bulstrode and Lacey – the Government representatives – have already sent one agent in, but he came back dead – poisoned with a quick-acting toxin that took two days to work.

'You're a horse with tits!'
Jeff to Marty

Jeff (pretending to be a research chemist with ten years' experience in cytogenetics) and Jeannie (degrees in maths, physics and bionics) apply for jobs with The Pain Corporation. Its laboratories are located rather oddly beneath a golf course and its head, Colonel Anger, is a broken man confined to a wheelchair. His aircraft crashed in the Amazonian jungle some twenty years before, and his life was saved by a nearby tribe of Indians. His office is filled with South American plants, he keeps the plane wreck somewhere off in the greenery, and one of the Indians is on hand continually to feed him Niaca – the herb that apparently keeps him healthy and which will only grow in the Amazonian jungle. And despite Anger's recreation of that jungle deep beneath England's green and pleasant land, he can't grow any more.

With Marty's help, Jeff and Jeannie discover that Anger died twenty years ago, but is keeping his death at arm's length using Niaca. When Wyvern realizes what Anger is doing, he is horrified. If nobody ever died, the world would quickly stagnate. Fear of death is what keeps civilization going.

Anger has been trying to discover how to manufacture a Niaca substitute, but has been unsuccessful in stabilizing the drug. Now aware of Marty's presence through Ramon's spiritual sensitivity, and of Marty's access to the secrets of the Afterlife, Anger tries to force the secret of successful Niaca propagation from Marty and Jeff. But, with his pure supply exhausted, Anger's long-delayed death finally catches up with him.

Although writer Gareth Roberts also co-scripted 'Whatever Possessed You', the first episode of the second series, the first work he did for the programme was 'Pain Killers'. He got the job through another writer of *Doctor Who* novels – Mark Gatiss from the comedy team *The League of Gentlemen*.

'What happened,' Gareth explains, 'was that Mark Gatiss had appeared in the first episode of

Below and opposite: Dervla Kirwan portrays Petra Winters, the scientist who falls for Jeff.
Above: *The useful and serious work of the Pain Corporation.*

the first series as a rising Britcom star, and he was working on writing for the second series with Jeremy Dyson. Charlie was looking for people to come in and lift the burden from his shoulders because he knew that he wouldn't be able to devote as much time to scripting the second series as he did the first. I think that one of the things Charlie said was, "I really need somebody that can do the fantasy *and* the relationship stuff," and a light bulb came on over Mark's head. I've known him for eight or nine years, and he knew I'd done *Doctor Who* novels and I'd done *Coronation Street, Emmerdale* and *Brookside*, so I could handle both. I went in to see Charlie, he showed me some ideas and we took it from there.'

Although Gareth wrote the script alone, the original premise was Charlie Higson's. 'What Charlie found from the first series,' says Gareth, 'was that it was better to concentrate the action in one place so you could set a unit up there and film it all very economically rather than tearing round the countryside doing different locations in different places. So he had a list of about seven or eight settings and ideas for stories which I think he'd already shown to the BBC when he was selling them the second series. The one I took for 'Pain Killers' was "There's a drug which delays pain in amusing and threatening ways, and it's set in a sinister scientific base." I'm happy with the idea of a sinister scientific base because they're a

staple of television and film science fiction so there's a lot of fun you can have.'

Gareth, like Higson, is fond of television series of the late 1960s and early 1970s: the era from which the new *Randall & Hopkirk (Deceased)* series sprang. His script for 'Pain Killers' is littered with little, knowing references to other television shows. The scene where Jeff and Jeannie are led through The Pain Corporation (originally known as the Brainbox) and see through round windows as a number of bizarre experiments are carried out is lifted from an episode of *The Prisoner*, for instance, whilst the image of Colonel Anger sitting at a desk in the middle of what appears to be the Amazonian rain forest parallels a similar shot in the *Doctor Who* story 'The Seeds of Doom'.

'The sort of references I put in were very oblique,' Gareth admits, rather guiltily, 'so if you didn't know you wouldn't know, and you're not expected to know, and if you do know then it just gives you a little chuckle as you go along. It's always the way with fandom that there are ten million people who will watch the programme and only twenty thousand who will buy the merchandise, so the rest of those people won't pick it up, and it shouldn't lessen their enjoyment at all, but it's fun for the rest of us. I think if you do it in a portentous way then it's a bit of a turn-off, but if you do it humorously then people quite enjoy it.'

One of the things the new *Randall & Hopkirk (Deceased)* has in common with its old ITC predecessors is the quality of the actors and actresses who appear in the episodes. Here one of Britain's finest actors – Sir Derek Jacobi – plays the villain, while Dervla Kirwan (formerly of *Ballykissangel*) appears as his assistant, Petra Winters, and comedy actor Duncan Preston (*Surgical Spirit*, *Dinnerladies* and Victoria Wood's spoof soap opera *Acorn Antiques*) plays the small but important role of Doctor Hickman.

Gareth was ecstatic at Jacobi's appearance in his episode. 'He is one of my favourite actors, and I dropped my chips when I heard that he'd been

cast.' Gareth had, however, originally been imagining someone quite different. 'When I was writing it I was thinking of Leo McKern's Number Two from *The Prisoner* – that kind of guy who wanders around showing you things and just being mysterious, and yet is also quite jovial and convivial but actually a very nasty person.'

The page of script for the scene where Jeff and Jeannie are led past the various laboratory windows in The Pain Corporation, and see something of the work being done by Colonel Anger's scientists, contains the description: *A team of scientists is clustered round a man in pyjamas playing with building blocks… (played by the writer if poss?).* It was, apparently, possible.

'I thought it would be fun to be one of those people you see through the windows, lurching about and doing something very odd,' Gareth explains, 'and I thought that as Charlie is always in the series, and Mark Gatiss is in it, I don't see any reason why I shouldn't make a cameo

appearance. I play a man who has been regressed to childhood by sinister scientists, and the costume department made me a lovely pair of teddy bear pyjamas with teddy bear buttons, which I was allowed to take home. I think I'm going to look like the maddest person the world has ever known. I didn't have any lines or anything, I just gurgled and played with an enormous teddy bear.'

As with all the episodes, the majority of the filming was done on location. According to Gareth, 'They used what I think was a disused Masonic School – the American University Campus in Hertfordshire. It had a drained swimming pool where I did my cameo, and also lots of nice soundproofed rooms which have nothing in them.' Nailing his fan colours firmly to the mast, he adds: 'The really exciting thing for me was driving up the drive and realizing that it was where the episode 'Death's Door' was filmed for *The Avengers*.'

Below: Colonel Anger (Sir Derek Jacobi) was saved by Ramon (Nitin Ganatra) when his aircraft crashed in the jungle, but his gratitude doesn't extend very far.
***Opposite:** The effects of the climactic fight scene from the episode are delayed by the painkiller Niarol, but catch up with both Jeff and Jeannie later.*

The sets in *Randall & Hopkirk (Deceased)* are an integral part of the 'feel' of the series. Rather than the standard pubs, hotel rooms and offices of the original 1960s version, Charlie Higson has always pushed for a level of surrealism, of fantasy, of something just across the edge.

'We did things on this series that I never thought we'd manage,' he admits, 'like an underground forest with a crashed plane in it.'

It wasn't a real wood, of course. But, special effects notwithstanding, they were real trees.

'The woods we were filming "The Glorious Butranekh" in, they clear trees all the time out of there,' explains Charlie. 'The designer went down and ordered up a whole load of trees, which they cut down and put up in the studio. It wasn't that expensive, because it was just trees, and then they got the plane for nothing from a dump. I was very pleased with that. There's things you think, oh we'll write it in but it'll never happen – we'll probably end up with a couple of pot plants and a few vines…'

Wyvern: 'Sorry – I was just being a little teapot. It's a terrible habit of mine.'

Marty: 'Why were you being a little teapot?'

Wyvern: 'It makes a change from being a little coffee pot.'

the glorious butranekh

Written by Charlie Higson. Directed by Charlie Higson

Above and right: *The Glorious Butranekh himself.*
Opposite: *Felia Siderova (here played by Pauline Quirke), Jeff and Jeannie's former receptionist. Charlie Higson named the character after a stage name once used by Hollywood legend (and one-time dancing partner of Fred Astaire) Cyd Charisse.*

There are people who wait for King Arthur to return in the hour of his country's greatest need. Unwilling to solve problems for themselves, they want someone else to do it for them. And if King Arthur doesn't come along in time, well, perhaps they might just go looking for him…

Jeannie takes a phone call from Felia – the receptionist who used to work for Marty and Jeff. She's back in her home country of Latvia with her baby, young Marty, and her husband Yuri, but both Yuri and baby Marty have disappeared. Felia thinks that someone is after her as well. Jeff and Jeannie are the only people she can turn to. Can they help?

They can indeed. The two of them fly immediately to Latvia, with a reluctant Marty in tow, and begin their investigations.

They find Felia in an old, abandoned theatre where she has gone to ground. She tells them that Yuri started acting oddly, shortly after she returned. He had money, although he had no job. He went out a lot, and would not tell her where he went. And he doted on baby Marty, but he paid her little attention.

Pretty soon Marty locates Yuri, bound and near death, in a secret room in Felia's apartment. He dies just as they get to him. It looks as if his blood has been drained, and it looks as if he didn't put up much of a struggle. It looks, in fact, as if he may have collaborated in his own death.

While Jeannie guards Felia, Yuri's last words lead Jeff and Marty to a nurse at the local hospital. She, in turn, points them towards a Russian Mafia bar where they bump into Pola Sunset, a model who follows the Butra cult – the belief that the glorious eleventh-century Latvian war hero Butranekh will be reborn to save the country from those who would bring it down – which is just about anyone, it would seem. Pola has wished to join them ever since she was a child, but never had the nerve. Until now.

Together, Jeff and Pola seek out the Butra in Latvia's forests, but the Butra reject Pola, killing her. Jeff, distraught over her death, heads into the forest, and the stronghold of the Butra. They capture him, and tell him that baby Marty is the reincarnation of Butranekh (whose corpse they have on display). Butranekh needs souls to assure his health, and Jeff's soul will do nicely.

Butra assassins arrive at the dilapidated theatre, having discovered Felia's location. They want her dead, severing the final link between baby Marty and his family. Together, Jeannie and Felia fight them off.

Marty, aided by Wyvern, finds Yuri in Limbo, and together they reanimate the corpse of Butranekh in the forest, terrifying the Butra and

telling them that the baby is just a baby, not a reincarnated warrior. The Butra disperse, and Jeff takes baby Marty back to Felia and Jeannie.

'The Glorious Butranekh', like 'Marshall and Snellgrove', picks up on ideas that were introduced in the first series.

'We were shooting a bit in Windsor Great Forest,' says Charlie Higson, 'and I thought, "Oh, a forest is a nice location." The plan for the second series was meant to be that, to balance up some of the more elaborate, expensive episodes, we would try and do some cheap ones. And I thought, "Okay, we'll do one set entirely in a forest, because it wouldn't cost us any money at all. We don't need to build any sets, it's quite atmospheric…" So I just had the idea of a couple of witches in a hut in a forest. And then I had the idea of bringing Felia back. I quite liked the idea of her baby being kidnapped, because it was set up as a plot element in the first series, where she has the baby and they both die and Marty brings them back from the dead.'

Problems arose close to filming when Jessica Stevenson (who played Felia in the first series) was unexpectedly offered another job. In Australia.

'Having thought she was available,' Charlie says, 'when it came to filming we discovered that she wasn't, so we had to recast. I was faced with three options. One: to take her out of the story altogether and make it someone else ringing them up and asking them to come to Latvia to find a baby, which was a route I didn't want to go down because it involved too much work at that late stage. Two: try to find a look-alike, possibly even a genuine Eastern European look-alike. Three: go with a star. Pauline Quirk was someone that Bob suggested. At first I was upset that we couldn't get Jessica back, but when I realized we could have Pauline Quirk I was ecstatic.'

Filming Latvia within an hour's drive of central London is not the easiest process in the world, and Production Designer Simon Waters had to approach the task in a slightly different manner from usual. The Butra's headquarters, for instance, were built twice – once in the studio for the

Filming for the forest scenes in 'The Glorious Butranekh' was almost cancelled due to the Foot and Mouth crisis affecting the area. As it was, stringent procedures had to be put in place to disinfect the cast and crew when they arrived on location.

Opposite right: *A storyboard sequence shows the reanimation of the Glorious Latvian warrior Butranekh.*

interior shots and once in Farnham Forest for the exterior shots. Both times, Simon used the same rather unusual basis.

'It was a white plastic wedding marquee. Charlie ran into my office and said, "Simon, we can't have this – it's a white plastic wedding marquee! I want an ethnic Latvian tent." I said, "Don't panic, don't panic, you won't recognize it."'

The process of turning a white plastic marquee into a Latvian tent took about a day.

'We opened the sides up,' Simon explains, 'and put poles up, so that rather than being a square, it started to be a square with little avenues and shapes off it. The outside was white plastic but the inside we draped with carpets and old poles. We unlaced one side of the roof and put some muslin across so we could get some nice light filtering across the tent. I said to the set decorator, "I want thirty old tarpaulins, I want forty-five faded carpets, some bits of hessian, some brown paint…" I put quite a lot of corrugated iron in there, with some Latvian posters that we had printed up, stuck to the corrugated iron and torn off, so you could see little bits of Latvian graphics. That sort of set, it's an instinctive thing. It would be very difficult to brief anybody about it. I knew in my mind what it would be like. It evolves, you create it like a sculpture. Sets like that are great fun to do.'

two can play at that game

Written by Mark Gatiss and Jeremy Dyson. Directed by Steve Bendelack

Below: Jeannie interrupts a meeting with her stationery supplier, Helium Harry (Reece Shearsmith) to help Stuart Boyle (John Michie).
Right: Helium Harry helps Jeff (and Marty) follow Jeannie's trail. And he can get Jeff a great deal on some gel pens.
Opposite: Jeannie and Stuart get into trouble in Boyle's Department Store, but luckily Jeff comes to the rescue.

School days. Cross-country runs. Desks incised with names of old pupils. Blu-Tack and yellowing sticky tape on the walls. The things that happened to you at school stay with you for the rest of your life…

While Jeff is recovering from an injury, Jeannie takes on a case. Stuart Boyle, an old school friend of Jeff's, has received a note from his father asking for a meeting at the old – and now derelict – department store the family own. The problem is: Stuart's father has been dead for six years, having apparently committed suicide when the store was going through a bad patch. Jeannie arranges to meet Stuart at the department store in order to provide Stuart with moral support at the meeting, but she is kidnapped and drugged by a mysterious figure when she arrives.

Jeff and Marty are going through a bad patch. During a particularly vicious argument, Marty finds himself unable to talk to Jeff, and Jeff

realizes that he can no longer see Marty.

Jeannie wakes up in a surreal, distorted version of a department store perfume department. She and Stuart are both tied to chairs. A mannequin attempts to spray acid in her face, but she manages to duck out of the way. The acid eats through Stuart's bonds, and together they escape into the strangely redesigned interior of the store.

In Limbo, Wyvern warns Marty that he is at a moment of spiritual crisis, estranged from his partner and at risk from dark forces that are manoeuvring to take advantage of his weakness. Marty finds himself in Rhadamanthus-on-Sea: a place for suddenly single spirits to 'get their act together'. It just happens to look like Eastbourne on a wet afternoon. Marty falls in with Dicky Klein (of the comedy duo D. Klein and Fall), but there is something not quite right about this faded comedian.

Jeff, realizing that Jeannie has gone missing, tracks her to Boyle's Department Store, and joins her and Stuart in their attempt to escape from whatever malevolent presence is manipulating the store and its contents.

In Rhadamanthus-on-Sea, Marty discovers that spirits who have lost their partners are left to rot, alone on the pier. Fighting against the

forces which are attempting to keep him there – given form as Dicky Klein and the boarding house landlady, Mrs Applegarth – Marty wishes desperately that he could apologize to Jeff.

Penetrating the heart of the eerie department store, Jeff and Jeannie discover that Stuart is controlling everything, and always has been since he killed his father. He lured them there so that he could take his revenge on Jeff for being the boy who was only just ahead of him in all the athletic events. During a climactic computer game, Jeff desperately wishes that he could apologize to Marty.

The force of their simultaneous apologies pulls the ghost and his mortal friend back together, united again in friendship. Marty uses his powers to throw Stuart into a giant computer screen, where he is electrocuted.

Writers Mark Gatiss and Jeremy Dyson are better known as part of The League of Gentlemen: the award-winning stand-up comedy partnership who created the nightmarish village of Royston Vasey for their stage, TV and radio shows.

Dyson himself has given up acting, but Gatiss appeared as Inspector Large in 'Drop Dead', the very first episode. Steve Pemberton, third Gentleman from the League, appeared in the same episode as Sergeant Liddel, and Reece Shearsmith, fourth and last of the Gentlemen, makes a cameo appearance in this episode as Jeannie and Jeff's stationery supplier, Helium Harry.

'I've always loved their writing,' enthuses Charlie Higson. 'They are fantastic at characters, and that bizarre comedy-horror they like, so I felt they would be good to write at least an episode. They also have such strong, memorable female characters, but in their first-draft script Jeannie was hardly in it. I said, "What's happened to Jeannie?" and they said, "Well, we can only write for men dressed up as women." So I said, "Imagine that's what she is."'

As it turned out, Gatiss and Dyson came up with what was generally considered to be a fantastic first script, most of which was just not possible within the show's budget.

'I was having to steer it towards what I knew we could achieve without losing too much of their original dream,' Charlie continues. 'We did it late in shooting, and the director – Steve Bendelack – came on board quite late, and by then we'd run out of money.'

Charlie illustrates this with an example from the script, where Jeff and Stuart are supposed to confront each other at the end in a race to the death in life-size Scalextric cars.

'I said, "Look, we're really not going to be able to afford this, can you think of something else?" So they came up with a big board game. I had a production meeting with the special-effects people, and we were talking about how we were going to achieve that, and I said, "You should see what they originally wanted to do – it was this life-size Scalextric set." And everybody's ears pricked up, and they said, "Wow, that would be fantastic…" So I said, "Alright, if that's what you want to do, let's do it." But of course as the day got nearer, and the practicalities of what we could film…' He shrugs. 'It was getting impossible. It was the sort of thing that, if you only half pull it off, it could have looked very, very sad. So at the last minute we had to change it yet again. We went back to one of their original ideas, which was to go from a massive idea for a fight to the death to a ridiculously small idea, which was a game of Pong – one of the very first computer games. And I suggested we make it a fifty-foot-high game of Pong.'

Guest stars in this episode are Roy Hudd and Eleanor Bron – comedy actors from two very different disciplines. Hudd, who has been presenting his radio show *The News Huddlines* for longer than most people can remember, is a true descendent of the old Music Hall tradition, whereas Bron emerged from the Cambridge

Footlights and has since carved a reputation for sharp, acerbic humour. They both perform star turns here.

'I'd wanted to work with director Steve Bendelack for a long time,' Charlie says. 'I loved what he did on *The League of Gentlemen*, particularly the Christmas special. He was very good on the visual side of things and also on special effects, and I thought he might bring the required madness and scope to the series. For a long time he wasn't sure if he wanted to do it. We had the fall-back option that I could do it if necessary, and there was the possibility that Rachel Talalay might be able to come back. Also, while Mark Mylod didn't want to commit to anything long term, because of the *Ali G* film, we thought he might be able to do one episode if he had the time. As it turned out, he didn't.'

Mark Gatiss and Gareth Roberts (writer of 'Pain Killers' and co-writer of 'Whatever Possessed You') both served their literary apprenticeships writing original novels based on the BBC's *Doctor Who* series. It's no surprise, therefore, to find them smuggling little references into their scripts. Here Gatiss manages a nod towards various *Doctor Who* stories, including 'The Hand of Fear' and 'Death to the Daleks' (the villainous mastermind is actually a desiccated corpse), 'Spearhead from Space' (department-store mannequins come to life) and 'The Daemons' (a heat barrier makes wooden objects explode). The script also contains echoes of *The Avengers*, particularly the episodes 'Death at Bargain Prices' and 'Dead Man's Treasure' – a debt acknowledged by Helium Harry's location in Steed Street…

> *Beware the idle tongue of wrath,*
> *That with malice makes thee scoff,*
> *For should thee thy chosen one deny,*
> *Thy soul is risked for all eternit-eye.*

'First floor: leisure wear, gentlemen's shoes, confusion, frustration and ultimate despair!'
Boyle's in-store announcement

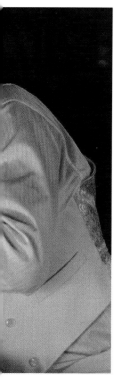

Opposite: Eleanor Bron (left) as Mrs Applegarth and Roy Hudd (right) as Dicky Klein.
Above right: In Rhadamanthus, Marty is encouraged to forget his Chosen One…
Right: …while in Boyle's store, Stuart seems to have gone ever so slightly mad.

epilogue

The date is Friday 23 March 2001; the place is Alice Holt Forest, a few miles away from the historic market town of Farnham in Surrey.

It's the last day of shooting for series two of *Randall & Hopkirk (Deceased)*. There remain weeks, if not months, of editing and digital effects work to complete, but as far as the actors are concerned, this is it. If they haven't got it on film by now, they won't get it on film at all.

A week ago the shooting was almost called off, thanks to the foot-and-mouth crisis currently affecting the countryside.

Two days ago, it snowed.

Yesterday it rained almost continuously.

Today there's a fine mist of rain in the air. Also in the air is what sounds like half the Army Air Corps, transferring men and equipment between the various military bases in this part of England.

You would be forgiven for thinking that Charlie Higson – the writer, producer and, most importantly at the moment, director of this final episode – has every right to be stamping up and down and shouting at people. In fact, he's actually smiling cheerfully as he tells Bob Mortimer to walk away from the camera, down a rutted track and into a patch of special-effects mist. The filming appears to have gone well.

Bob is carrying a small baby in his arms. It's a real baby, rather than a special effect, and when Charlie calls 'Cut!' in his mild, slightly tentative voice, Bob walks out of the mist and back toward the camera, swinging the baby around, dancing with it and making it laugh.

Off to one side, Vic Reeves is prowling around, scowling at his script as if he's never seen it before. Which, in fact, he hasn't.

'You're the first to know this,' he says conspiratorially, 'but I've done a controlled experiment on this episode by not reading any of the script. I want to see what it looks like when it's all put together without me actually knowing what is going on. I just read the pages every day. Tom [Baker] does that – he doesn't have a clue what he's doing. He says he only reads his bits and turns up and does them, so he doesn't know what he's going on about most of the time.'

Pine-cones crunch underfoot. Birds sing in the distance. Two special-effects men wander around topping up the fake mist. It doesn't feel like the last day of shooting.

Having finished his scene and returned the small child to its mother, Bob wanders across to join Simon and Vic. All three of them gaze calmly at the surreal sight of a Latvian tent sitting in the middle of an English forest, and beside it an altar made of old washing machines. The mist wraps itself around this makeshift 'camp'. People armed to the teeth are moving through the trees, swathed in long leather coats and fur hats; combined with the presence of a single figure suited and booted from head to toe all in white, there's a definite sense of mystery in the air. Not your usual film set for a detective series.

'All the stuff now seems to be your *Morse*s and your *Silent Witness*es,' Bob observes, quietly. 'It's all very earnest. But there's always a market for a bit of hocus-pocus. Something that doesn't take itself too seriously.'

Simon and Vic nod as, in the background, Charlie starts setting up for the final shot of the series.

the crew

Executive Producer	Simon Wright
Producer	Charlie Higson
Directors	Mark Mylod
	Charlie Higson
	Rachel Talalay
	Metin Huseyin
	Steve Bendelack
Writers	Charlie Higson
	Gareth Roberts
	Paul Whitehouse
	Mark Gatiss
	Jeremy Dyson
	Kate Wood
Director of Photography	John Ignatius
Production Designers	Grenville Horner (Series One)
	Simon Waters (Series Two)
Editors	Annie Kocur
	Brian Dyke
	David Hill
	Ronan Hyder
Visual Effects	Double Negative
Visual Effects Supervisors	Matthew Holben
	Fay McConkey
	Charlie Noble
	Antony Bluff
Music	Murray Gold
Theme Music	David Arnold and Tim Simenon
Line Producers	Liz Bunton (Series One)
	Josh Dynever (Series Two)
Casting Director	Marilyn Johnson
Associate Producer	Analisa Barreto
First Assistant Directors	Ken Shane (Series One)
	Dean Byfield (Series Two)
	Jay Arthur (Series Two)
Sound Recordist	Steve Phillips
Boom Operator	Jeff Milner
Chief Make-Up	Jane Walker
Make-Up Artist	Jayne Buxton
Costume Designer	June Nevin
Supervising Sound Editor	Colin Chapman
Second Assistant Directors	Trevor Puckle (Series One)
	Sasha Mann (Series Two)
	Peter Nightingale (Series Two)
Third Assistant Directors	Janine Law (Series One)
	Grenville Bartlett (Series Two)
	Kerry Green (Series Two)
Location Managers	Pat Karam (Series One)
	Kas Braganza (Series Two)
Assistant Location Managers	Giles Edleston (Series One)
	Jay Harradine (Series Two)
	Annie East (Series Two)
	Jeff Golding (Series Two)
Unit Manager	Tracey Tucker (Series One)
Production Accountants	Susanna Wyatt (Series One)
	Sarah Kaye (Series Two)
Assistant Accountants	Lynne Greenshields (Series One)
	Rica Seeto (Series Two)
Production Co-ordinators	Ruta Ozols (Series One)
	Amanda Wilkie (Series Two)
Assistant to Charlie Higson	Sophie Siegle
Publicist	Frances Pardell
Production Runner	Matt Yelland (Series Two)

Production Secretaries	Natasha Gormley (Series One)
	Rebecca Nazareth (Series Two)
Script Supervisors	Julie Brown (Series One)
	Jemma Field (Series Two)
Camera Operators	Peter Versey (Series One)
	Martin Foley (Series Two)
Steadycam Operators	Roger Tooley
	Alf Tramontin
	Rupert Power
Focus Pullers	Ben Wilson (Series One)
	Adam Coles (Series Two)
Clapper/Loaders	Ian Struthers (Series One)
	Jamie Southcott (Series Two)
	Dave McDowell (Series Two)
Camera Grips	Andy Kendall (Series One)
	Ronan Murphy (Series Two)
Wardrobe Mistress	Sharon Robinson (Series One)
Costume Supervisor	Alison Wyldeck (Series Two)
Wardrobe Assistant	Pookie Russell (Series One)
Costume Assistant	Celia Yau (Series Two)
Art Directors	Sarah Kane (Series One)
	David Walley (Series One)
	Anna Deamer (Series Two)
	Lucy Dummer (Series Two)
Art Directors on Camera	Madelaine Leech
	Amanda Craggs (Series Two)
Storyboard Artist	Mike Nicholson
Production Buyers	Ian Tulley (Series One)
	Peter Rutherford (Series Two)
Property Masters	Trevor Daniels
	Paul Kearney (Series Two)
Dressing Props	Simon Buret
	Noel Deegan
	Brian Pincham (Series Two)
	Patrick Duncan-Burgess (Series Two)
Standby Props	Eric Levy
	Barry Howard Clark
	John Grimwood (Series One)
Construction Manager	David Bubb (Series Two)
Standby Carpenters	Mike Eager (Series One)
	Dave Gibson (Series Two)
Standby Painter	Dave Stapleton
Standby Rigger	Martin Goddard
Gaffer	George Vince
Best Boy	Andy Hebden (Series One)
	Chris Bryan (Series Two)
Electricians	Kenny Redford (Series One)
	Rick Loughlin (Series One)
	John Sturt (Series Two)
	Alex Swinton (Series Two)
	Colin Price (Series Two)
Special Effects	Artem Visual Effects (Series One)
	Special Effects GB (Series Two)
Armourers	Perdix Firearms
Stunt Co-ordinator	Rod Woodruff
Titles	Tomato Design
Music Supervisor	Nick Angel
Sound Editors	Joe Gallagher
	Brigitte Arnold
	Paul McFadden
	Mike Feinberg
Re-Recording Mixer	Alan Snelling
Telecine Operator	Adrian Seery
Assistant Editors	Gez Morris
	Ronan Hyder (Series One)

merchandise

Various spin-off products have kept fans happy during the gap between series one and series two. There's the soundtrack album which contains a vocal version of David Arnold's theme tune (sung by Nina Persson of the Cardigans) and many of the songs that were recorded for the show, and there are also two original spin-off novels.

Ghost of a Chance, by Graeme Grant, picks up on a throwaway reference that Charlie Higson made to Marty's past in the pre-production notes for series one. Higson had imagined that Marty had always wanted to be a night-club singer, and had once been involved with a gangster's girlfriend while singing in the clubs. Grant then wove a story around these 'facts' in which the girlfriend returns, seeking Marty's help in finding a mutual friend.

Andy Lane's *Ghost in the Machine* takes a more fantastical slant, with Jeff hired to investigate the slaying and flaying of a Scottish millionaire and becoming involved in a plot that concerns robotic submarines, Russian hit-squads and Israeli agents.

Both books are still available, and further information on the series, including interviews and behind-the-scenes information, can be found on the official *Randall & Hopkirk (Deceased)* website: **www.randallandhopkirk.org.uk**

picture acknowledgements

Joss Barratt 4–5, 9, 10 (bottom), 11, 12–13, 15, 16, 17, 18 (bottom), 19 (bottom), 20 [2, 3 & 6], 21 (main picture), 46, 50–51, 54, 56, 62 (bottom), 63, 64, 71, 72, 83 (bottom two pictures), 90 (left), 91 (both pictures), 92 (bottom middle and right), 93 (both pictures), 118 (top), 119, 120, 121 (bottom), 122–30, 131 (top), 132, 133 (top), 134, 135 (both pictures), 136–8, 140–41 (all pictures), 142 (bottom), 143

Carlton International Media Limited © 1969 and 2001. All rights reserved 22–3, 25 (both pictures)

Justin Canning 57, 62 (top), 83 (top), 92 (left) 150, 164–5, 167 (bottom), 168 (top left and right, bottom left), 169 (top)

Grenville Horner 81

Steve Lovell Davis 73, 75, 151 (all pictures), 190–91 (all pictures)

Jim Moir 10 (top left), 26 (bottom), 49 (bottom), 55, 58, 90 (right), 99 (left), 166, 168 (bottom right), 186 (left)

Gary Moyes 7, 10 (top right), 19 (top), 20 [1], 28–9, 31, 42 (top), 43, 44–5, 48 (both pictures), 52–3, 59, 60–61, 66, 67 (all pictures), 68–9, 74 (bottom), 96–7, 98, 100 (top), 101 (both pictures), 116–17, 149 (top), 152–63 (all pictures), 170–75, 177–81, 183 (both pictures), 184 (top sequence), 185 (top left), 186 (right), 187 (top), 188–9 (all pictures)

Dan Newman 84 (both), 85 (top), 87 (top right)

Adrian Rogers 47, 92 (top right), 146–8 (all pictures)

Tomato Design (Graham Woods) 94–5

Brian Tonks 18 (top), 20 [4], 99 (right), 133 (bottom)

Simon Waters 26 (top), 76–7, 80 (bottom), 85 (bottom), 86 (top), 87 (top left)

Nick West 118 (bottom)

Brian Williams 121 (artworks)

WTTV Ltd 20 [5 & 7], 21 (insets), 24, 27 (all pictures), 30, 32–3 (all pictures), 34, 36–7 (all pictures), 38–9 (all pictures), 40–41 (all pictures), 42 (bottom), 49 (top), 74 (top), 86 (bottom), 87 (bottom), 100 (middle and bottom), 103, 104–105, 106–15 (all pictures), 131 (middle and bottom), 139 (top), 141 (top), 144 (both pictures), 145, 149 (bottom), 167 (top), 169 (bottom), 176, 182, 184 (bottom), 185 (top right and bottom), 187 (bottom)

All storyboard sketches provided by Mike Nicholson and costume sketches by June Nevin.